THIN ICE

THIN ICE

CALLIE HART™ BOOK ONE

RENÉE JAGGÉR

LMBPN PUBLISHING

Copyright © 2020 Renée Jaggér
Cover by Cover by Fantasy Book Design
Cover copyright © LMBPN Publishing

LMBPN Publishing
PMB 196, 2540 South Maryland Pkwy
Las Vegas, NV 89109

First US edition, April 2020
Print ISBN: 978-1-64202-870-6

CHAPTER ONE

I rounded the corner and pulled my gun...on another mannequin. Damn, I hated working the night shift. The flashlight beam danced over the featureless plastic body, stopping on a pair of bright blue boxers with a yellow waistband. A sign next to the display bragged about all the awards Kloud9 underwear had won over the last few years. Who the heck gave underwear awards anyway?

The radio clipped to my chest crackled to life. "Everything okay in there, rookie? You need backup?" Amusement laced my shift partner's voice.

I put my gun back in its holster and swept the flashlight up and to the right, stopping when the beam hit the camera in the corner to raise a middle finger. "Screw you, Ted."

He was probably laughing his ass off in the guard shack. Who could blame him? If I was in his shoes, I'd be laughing at the jumpy rookie security guard too.

"Watch out for those UltraComfort Briefs, Callie. They'll get ya every time." Ted snickered into the radio.

Dammit, I just knew he'd play the footage for my boss,

Eddie, in the morning, and the two of them would have a big laugh at my expense. They were a bunch of dicks, but it was all in fun. I'd get back at them when I got a chance. I wouldn't be the rookie forever.

"Laugh it up, Ted. Just wait 'til I get back there," I growled. The radio squealed when I let go of the talk button.

Ted got serious. "Better wrap up your round soon, Callie. Sounds like your radio needs new batteries, and I'd hate for you to get stranded on the factory floor with those mannequins. They're creepy as hell in the dark."

"Almost done. Be back in a few." I sighed and walked around the mannequin, then up the stairs to the offices.

Fucking jokers. Everyone played pranks on each other. Ted was an okay guy, and I didn't mind working with him most days. Not someone I'd choose to hang out with after hours, but that applied to the rest of the guards as well. Most of them were older than my dad, retirees with past military or police experience. Given the pay, no one would want the job except pensioners and broke millennials. Guarding an underwear factory wasn't in-demand employment. I didn't even know why they needed guards, but I wasn't about to turn down the paycheck. Mine was not to reason why.

I'd left the day shift the week before, and I was the rookie on graveyard. As such, I was the butt of every joke. It was a rite of passage, one I'd have to endure if I wanted the pay bump that came with the overnight shift.

One more year, maybe two, then I'm out of here. I just need relevant experience to find better work is all. I swept the narrow flashlight beam over the cubicles and the executive boardroom to my right. During the day, everything would've been illuminated by buzzing fluorescent lights, but at night, it was dark up here except for the few emergency lights. The shadows were long, and all the familiar fixtures seemed like strangers. I blamed that, plus my insomnia, for my jumpiness. The change in sleep schedules would do that to anyone—or that was what I told myself. At least there were no mannequins up here, so maybe I wouldn't stroke out just yet.

I breathed a sigh of relief as I completed my rounds on the office floor of the factory and went back outside. The naked limbs of the old oak tree waved at me from where it leaned over the building. It'd shed the last of its leaves over the weekend, and they had been raked into a pile at the edge of the parking lot, along with a fallen tree branch. There was a bunch of sticks out of the pile.

The blacktop glistened from the recent rainfall, and my breath came out in a cloud. If the temperature dropped much more, the lot would get icy. I'd have to remember to tell Ted to salt the sidewalks and pick up the fallen sticks before the morning shift came on. It was the least he could do to make up for laughing at me.

I was just about to start for the guard shack when a sliver of light caught my eye. I turned, running the flashlight over the factory wall to my right. The emergency exit was open, and the light I'd seen was coming from within.

That shouldn't be open. I took a step toward it but stopped. Company policy said the security guards weren't to investigate potential intrusions on their own. I was supposed to call back to the shack, alert Ted, and wait for him to show up.

"Ted," I whispered into the radio, but it didn't make the normal static sound that told me we were connected. With a curse, I yanked the radio off my chest and examined it. The ready light was out. "Dammit, of all the times for my batteries to die!"

Twin bangs rang through the cold air, the unmistakable sound of gunshots, and they'd come from the other side of the open gate.

I was out of time; I couldn't wait for Ted to show up. I sprinted toward the door, my gun in my hand, and pressed my back to the wall beside it, making myself as small as I could. There wasn't much to see when I peeked in except for some light material billowing in the breeze coming through the door. Voices drifted to me, though—mostly grunts and muffled cursing— and also the sounds of a struggle. I pushed the door open with the barrel of my gun and spun into the opening, weapon in front of me, breathing steady, focused, and calm, just like they'd taught me in Basic.

Shapes moved on the other side of the material, dark humanoid shadows. Why the hell had it been hung from the ceiling in this area? I stepped through a gap between two of them. White sheets had been hung all around to form a small room, and the sheet opposite me was splashed with blood. Bright lights on tripods occupied the corner near me. One of them had been knocked over and broken in the struggle. A guy in a suit sat on the floor near the man who'd been shot, while two other men wrestled for a gun halfway between us. It felt like minutes had passed since I'd entered the enclosure, but that was the adrenaline talking. My reaction was near-instant. I raised my gun, pointed it at the man with the weapon, and shouted, "Put down the weapon, or I'll shoot!"

He shifted the gun, pressed it to the other man's temple, and fired.

I squeezed the trigger but my shot went wide, just grazing the gunman's arm. He dropped the weapon, but it was too late for the other man. At least, that was what I thought as I went over to check him.

"No, don't!" the gunman shouted, but I was already there.

The guy who had just taken a bullet to the head sat up and lunged at me. I fired at him by instinct while backing up, which did me no good. He sprang to his feet impossibly fast, his body jerking as the bullets hit him in the chest. I shot him four times almost point-blank, but he didn't slow down or stop. His face twisted as a second set of teeth sprouted from his jaws, stretching into fangs.

What the hell?

He sprang toward me.

Time slowed, and the details of the scene before me suddenly came into focus. The first injured man, the one on the floor near the suit with the VIP badge, was bleeding profusely from the neck. At first, I'd thought he'd been shot, but now I wasn't so sure. It looked like a huge chunk of flesh was missing, and the edges were jagged. I wondered why Ted hadn't told me someone else was on the property. He had to have known since the one guy had a visitor badge.

For a second, I felt like I was falling through time. I saw friends half a world away. Friends with their throats torn out. Dead friends with dog tags and enough firepower to level a small city. Something had gotten to them, and whatever it was, it was fast—too fast for anyone to get off a shot.

The memory flashed through my mind, gone as quickly as it had come, but the fanged monster was still closing on me.

I tried to fire again but the monster slammed into me, pushing us through the sheets and out the door.

I landed on my back with a grunt and a thud and the rabid monster on top of me. He slashed at me with his fingernails, then lunged at my throat, snapping his teeth. It was all I could do to keep my arms up to defend myself.

I had to get the upper hand. I turned my head, searching for my gun, but the damn thing was out of reach. Besides, I'd just unloaded multiple bullets into this psychopath, and he hadn't even noticed. I needed a different weapon, but this was a damn parking lot. There *was* nothing else.

The creature let up for a fraction of a second, long enough for me to pull one arm away. I held him back with the other, but he was strong. I wouldn't be able to keep him off me for long. My free hand swept across the wet pavement, searching for anything I could use to give myself the advantage. My fist closed around something rough that was about three inches in diameter, and I swung it and hit the monster in the side of the head.

He didn't let me go, but the blow was enough to stun him for a minute. He loosened his grip on me enough that I was able to push him back. I reached for the gun, but he lunged at me again before I was able to grab it. I screamed and instinctively thrust the broken end of the stick at him.

He froze as the point entered his chest, eyes wide. The strange teeth sank back into his jaws, and his body went limp.

He was dead. I suddenly felt sick at the realization and pushed him off me.

When his body hit the ground, it was already stiff, as if he'd been dead for hours. The stick still protruded from his chest. He lay on his back, limbs curled up like a dead spider's, for a second, maybe two, before he disintegrated into dust.

A sound echoed through the parking lot, bouncing off the pavement and the side of the building. I turned to find the VIP in the suit standing in the emergency exit, applauding me.

Footsteps splashed through puddles as Ted rushed around the side of the building, red-faced, his hand on his gun. He stopped to gulp a breath of air, eyes moving wildly from me to the pile of dust to the VIP. "Callie, what the hell happened here?"

"That's a good question." I glanced at what was left of the guy who'd attacked me. There wasn't enough to identify. *What the hell was that thing?*

"I'm calling this in." Ted pulled out his phone to call the cops.

I tipped my head toward the sky and groaned. So much for the rest of my night.

CHAPTER TWO

An hour later, flashing red and blue lights bathed the outside of the Kloud9 Underwear factory. Three police cruisers, two ambulances, and a fire truck had wound up responding to Ted's emergency call. Don't ask me why the fire truck came. Must've been a slow night for house fires in Columbus. I wasn't going to complain about the eye candy, even if I did have to suffer through giving my testimony to the cops over and over.

"Ow." I flinched as the paramedic dabbed more alcohol on the tiny cut on my forehead. All I wanted was to go home, crawl into my bed, and forget all this had ever happened. Before I could do that, though, I had to sit through getting patched up and answer the police's repetitive questions. At least the medical care came at the company's expense. I sure couldn't afford to pay for it.

"Mrs. Hart," the cop in front of me said impatiently.

I had to stop myself from automatically correcting him to specialist. What the hell was wrong with me? I'd been out of the service for almost three years now. It was that Pthing. Fighting it had left me more shaken than I expected. "It's 'Miss.'"

He ignored my correction. "Back to your statement. You said the man who attacked you turned to dust?"

I rolled my eyes. "Do we have to go over this again? I know how it sounds, but I'm not crazy. Ask Ted and the other guy. They'll tell you the same thing."

He made a note in his little book.

The paramedic slapped a band-aid on my forehead and grabbed my arm to look at the cuts and scrapes there. I spied my boss Eddie chatting with another cop and pulled my arm away, sitting up straighter. The last thing I wanted was to look like I was incapable in front of him. I already looked incompetent, considering I had shot at an innocent man and another had died on my shift.

"Are we done here?" I asked, pulling the thin emergency blanket they'd given me up over my shoulders. "I gave you guys my statement already, and no offense, but I don't think my scrapes and bruises are going to be fatal."

The EMT nodded. "I'm finished."

The cop frowned at me.

I sighed. "Are you going to arrest me?"

"You're free to go." He grunted and waved me off.

I hopped down from the ambulance to talk to my boss. "Eddie, I'm glad you're here. Did you see the report?"

Eddie's white hair gleamed under the flashing lights as he ran his fingers through it. "I did."

"Then you know I made the best possible decisions based on the information I had at the time."

"That's not the point, Callie."

"I know company policy is to wait for backup, but if I had, we'd have four bodies instead of one."

He sighed and put a hand on my shoulder, leading me away from the police. "I know that. As far as I'm concerned, you did the right thing. Sadly, it's not up to me."

"But—"

"I'm just middle management, Callie. EEG Security is a big company with international shareholders. This comes from the top."

My heart sank to my toes. "Am I fired?"

He pressed his lips together and tilted his head in a way that made his crow's feet look deeper. "Officially, I was told to put you on unpaid leave. Felix is going to take your shifts for a while."

"When can I come back to work?"

The look on Eddie's face told me everything I needed to know. This wasn't a temporary layoff to let the heat die down.

He patted my back. "Between you and me, I'd update my resume just in case. And who knows? This could be a good thing. You're still young. There's plenty of opportunity out there, just waiting for you." He patted my back again and walked off when another officer called him.

I stood in the dark, staring at my shoes, the cold sinking into my bones. His words were meant to be comforting, but I didn't find them reassuring. Columbus was a big city, but there weren't many well-paying jobs for someone without a college degree. I supposed I could look into the manufacturing sector, but that would be awful, soul-sucking work. I hadn't taken the security job just for the money. I wanted to keep people safe. That was more important to me than a paycheck, even if my utility bills disagreed.

"Ms. Hart?"

I turned and found myself face to face with the VIP from earlier. In all the commotion, I hadn't gotten his name, and I still didn't know what he had been doing in that room of the factory so late at night.

"Ronan McCalister." He extended his hand. Something about his smile struck me, and not in a good way. He had the sort of camera-ready smile that belonged to someone who was used to flashing it to get what he wanted.

I took his hand. "Callie Hart. How are your people?"

"The one you shot will pull through. Minor injury. The other one? Not so much."

"I'm sorry to hear that."

McCalister shrugged. "Don't be. It's not your fault. It's thanks to you my other bodyguard and I survived the attack."

I shifted the blanket on my shoulders, suddenly uncomfortable. "Yeah, well, no good deed goes unpunished. Seems upper management would rather I'd let that thing kill you. What was he?"

McCalister shoved his hands into the pockets of his long black coat. It was way too thin for the cold, but he didn't seem bothered. I was freezing. "How are your injuries?"

Avoiding the question, huh? This guy knows something. I realized I was absentmindedly rubbing one of the scratches on my arm and dropped my hand. "I'm fine, except for my pride. No offense, Mr. McCalister—"

He wrinkled his nose. "Ronan, please."

I sighed and rubbed my nose. It was getting tingly from the chill. "I'm in kind of a bad mood. I just spent the last hour being grilled by the cops, only to get fired for saving your ass. If you don't want to tell me what's going on, that's your business, but I'm tired." I stepped past him.

"Ms. Hart?"

I stopped and turned around.

Ronan pulled a business card out of his pocket and held it out to me.

"What's this?" I asked, taking it. I read the text aloud. "Ronan McCalister: model, actor, musician?"

"You sound like you're in the market for work, and I'm in need of a new head of security. If you're interested, that is." He offered me a tight smile and leaned closer. "Report to the address on the back at eight on Monday morning if you want to know more about the thing that attacked us here tonight."

I watched Ronan walk off into the night and frowned. The last guy was barely cold, and here he was, looking to fill the position. Not only that, but he was offering it to me, someone he'd only just met. That was definitely odd. Then again, what about the night wasn't?

CHAPTER THREE

By the time the cops released me from the scene, the sun was up. I dragged myself to my car and drove home through morning rush hour, hating every minute of it. The only thing I could think of was falling into bed and forgetting any of this had ever happened.

Columbus, Ohio wasn't what you'd call an exciting city unless your version of excitement was watching the evening news. Crime had been through the roof since the recession, and many parts of the city that used to be nice had fallen into disrepair.

The arena district, however, was close enough to downtown that things weren't that bad. Being in proximity to all the major public buildings and the Nationwide Arena meant the area had a constant police presence. Skyrocketing rent was slowly forcing most of the college kids out of the area, but it was still affordable if two or three people split the costs.

I lived in a brick loft on the edge of the Arena District. The six-floor building was one of those places that had a perpetual For Rent sign out front. People moved out almost as soon as they moved in. That was especially true at this time of year when they got their first heating bills. Lofts could be expensive to heat, and winter comes early in Ohio.

I parked in my designated spot next to my roommate's moped and trudged through the double doors into the lobby. The maintenance guy was in there with his wet-vac again, working on the carpet near the mailboxes. No matter how many times he cleaned it, it always smelled like damp dog and mushrooms there.

The loft I shared with my roommate was on the fourth floor, and I chanced a trip in the elevator. It only worked about fifty percent of the time, and today wasn't one of those days. I groaned and took the stairs instead.

I could hear the television playing from the hallway. The minute I slid my key into the door, the volume was turned down. I swung the door open on a big, open area with exposed metal pipes in the ceiling and red brick walls. There were only a few walls in the apartment that weren't brick, and that was because they'd been added by the developers who'd flipped the property from a warehouse to apartments.

My bedroom was off to the right behind one of those walls, my bed calling to me like a soothing song. As exhausted as I was, my stomach had other ideas and refused to be ignored, so I trudged over to the fridge. Leftover pizza, takeout of questionable origin... What's this? When did we have cake? Since I couldn't tell if the frosting was supposed to be green or if that was mold, I left the cake alone and settled for pizza. Cold pizza and beer, the breakfast, or in my case, dinner, of champions.

I closed the fridge and found a face with pink pigtails and stick-on stars on her cheeks staring back at me. My heart leapt into my throat and I almost dropped my pizza. "Dammit, Sam! You scared the hell out of me! I didn't hear you!"

"It's my new slippers. I bought them online." Sam beamed and wiggled their pink, bunny ear slippers at me. "I thought they'd be perfect for a feminine waxing day when I got them, and I was right. I should treat myself more often."

"At this rate, your closet's going to overflow into the living area." I sank into one of the ugly red chairs that served as our living room furniture and chewed on the pizza.

As far as roommates went, I couldn't complain about Sam. At least things were not boring. I never knew if I was coming home to feminine Sam, decked out in pink, or masculine Sam in a football jersey, ball cap, and jeans, or anything in between. Sam's preferred pronouns were they/them, which had taken me about a year to get used to. Once I adjusted to the oddity that was Sam Shoemaker, I couldn't imagine life any other way.

"So," said Sam, climbing onto the counter and sitting cross-legged, "you going to tell me what happened at work that's got you in such a bad mood?"

I groaned and rolled my head back. Of course, that'd make the news. "Don't remind me."

"Come on, Callie. It can't be that bad. You work at an

underwear factory. What, did someone draw dicks on the mannequins again?"

"No, Sam."

"Too bad." Sam popped the top on an energy drink, also pink. "There's nothing creepier than a bunch of naked, anatomically incorrect plastic people standing around."

I snorted. "Says the person who keeps a fake dick in their pants two weeks out of every month."

"It's called a prosthetic, and it makes me feel better." They chugged the energy drink like a frat boy gulps down a beer.

"A prosthetic penis," I grumbled. "Maybe that's what Eddie needs. It's the closest he'll ever come to growing a pair."

Sam let out a loud burp that echoed through the loft, then slid off the counter. "Callie, seriously. What happened?"

I studied the slice in my hand. "EEG fired me."

Sam swept in, wrapping their arms around my shoulders and squeezing me so tight I could barely breathe. "I'm so sorry, Callie! What a prick!"

"Sam," I gasped and patted their arm. "Air!"

"Oh, sorry." Sam backed off and sat on the floor in front of me, waving their bunny slippers back and forth. "You know, I think OSU security is looking for people. I can talk to them if you want."

I cringed at the idea of working for campus security. My boss would probably be five years younger than me. "Thanks, but no thanks, Sam. Actually, there was this guy at the scene who offered me a job."

"What kind of job?" They leaned forward and snatched the pizza crust out of my hand to nibble on it.

I considered how much I should tell them. It wasn't like anyone had asked me to keep quiet about what happened, and some of the story would make the nightly news.

Over the next few minutes, I relayed what'd happened at Kloud9 to Sam, reciting as many details as I could remember. I debated not telling them about how strange the attacker was, but the rest of the tale wouldn't make sense without describing his fangs, his speed, and how he'd disintegrated. "I'm telling you, Sam, he turned into dust and blew away. The cops probably don't buy it, though. They probably think I'm crazy."

"What about security footage?"

"Corrupted." I took a long pull from the beer. "No one's sure what happened to it. In any case, there's no record of what happened. I'm relying on this Ronan guy to corroborate my story."

"And did he?"

I shrugged. "He had no reason not to. After all, he was the one who offered me the job."

"You should take it." Sam stood and took the empty beer bottle from my hand, going to drop it in the trash.

"I'm not going to take a job I know nothing about from some guy I've just met. That's how people get murdered, Sam."

"Was he hot?"

I wrinkled my nose. "What?"

Sam rolled their eyes and snatched their laptop from their art desk in the corner. "What did you say his name was?"

I dug the card out of my pocket and flipped it over. "Ronan McCalister."

Sam sprang to their feet, bounded across the room to snatch the card from between my fingers, and returned to their laptop. "The best way to find out about anyone is to look up their social media. Ronan McCalister." Their keys clicked at a furious speed. "Holy hopping hand grenades, girl! You didn't tell me he was a model!" They spun the screen around to show me an Instagram photo of the guy from the warehouse posing shirtless on a beach.

I raised an eyebrow. "Seriously? So he's good with an Instagram filter. Look how bogus the post is. More hashtag than heartthrob, if you ask me."

"You're kidding! You're so going, Callie. You at least need to hear the job offer." They hopped up and placed their laptop back on the desk. "And I want to hear all about it tomorrow night when I get back from class. Promise me you'll go?"

"No promises." I swung my feet up over the side of the chair and sank farther into it.

Sam sighed and plodded toward the shower.

The minute the shower started running, I closed my eyes. Just a short nap, then I could drag myself to bed for a proper sleep. As soon as my eyes were shut, though, all I could see was the military triage building where they'd taken the others in my squad after it happened. They'd been torn up pretty badly while out on patrol, and some had their necks ripped open. The medics were saying it had been an animal attack, but I had been there with them. What I saw run off into the mountains definitely wasn't an animal. It'd moved on two legs, but it was too fast to be human—just like the creature that'd come after me in the warehouse.

I'd tried to tell my superiors, the MPs, and even a general who was on the base. For the first twenty-four hours after it happened, I told anyone who would listen what I had seen. I thought maybe if they knew what had attacked them, they could save the few who were still fighting for their lives.

After I'd given my testimony a handful of times, two military police escorted me to a small room and made me sit. A man in a suit and sunglasses came in to tell me I wasn't ever to speak of it again. He used phrases like "national security," "need-to-know basis," and "security clearance" like seasoning. By the end, he'd made it clear that if I told anyone else what I'd seen, I'd be in a lot of trouble.

"Report to the address on the back at eight on Monday morning if you want to know more about the thing that attacked us here tonight." That was what Ronan had said.

He had answers. He knew what that thing was, and he'd implied he'd be willing to share his information. All I had to do was show up. I didn't have to accept the job.

With a sigh, I got out of the chair to retrieve Ronan's business card from where Sam had left it on their desk. The least I could do was hear him out, right?

CHAPTER FOUR

T he doorbell woke me on Monday morning. I groaned and rolled over in bed, sliding my feet into my slippers as it rang again. Delivery boy was early...again. "Dammit, Sam. If you're going to order stuff online, the least you could do is answer the door when it comes."

The bell kept ringing as I shrugged on my robe and dragged myself to the front door. A black-haired boy with a nose piercing smiled at me when I opened it. "Package for Sam!" He thrust a plain white box at me. "Hi, Callie. How're you?"

I grumbled something about being fine and grabbed the box. "You know, you could just leave it outside the door."

"Company policy. Someone has to pick it up. Oh, and I need a signature."

Ugh. Morning people. He was way too happy to be delivering packages that early. I scrawled my signature on his clipboard and gave it back to him with the pen.

"Thanks. Hey, tell Sam I said—"

"Yep." I closed the door and picked up the box, turning

it over in my hands. There wasn't a sender name anywhere on it. *What did you order this time, Sam?* I was curious and still too tired to be polite, so I dropped the box on the kitchen counter and cut the tape with a nearby knife.

"Mornin'." Sam yawned. Their slippers flopped against the cold floor as they made their way to the fridge. "Did I miss the delivery boy?"

"Yep." I opened the box. As soon as I peered into it, I wished I hadn't. "Ugh! Seriously, Sam? Warn a girl next time you order one of those." I pushed the box away.

Sam set aside the orange juice they'd just poured to grab the box. Their face lit up. "Hey, my new prosthetic is here!"

"That's the new prosthetic?" I cringed. "I thought those were supposed to mimic the real thing?"

"It does, see?" They lifted the largest prosthetic penis I'd ever seen from the box and waved it around. "I had it custom-made!"

I watched it bounce from side to side and was suddenly very glad I hadn't had breakfast yet. "In what universe are they naturally that size?"

Sam stopped bouncing it and rubbed their chin. "Hm. Good point. I think I ordered it on a waxing masculine day. Maybe got a bit overconfident." Sam dropped it back in the box and hugged the box to their chest. "You know, if you don't want to find a box with a dick in it, maybe you shouldn't open packages that are not addressed to you."

"Good point." I pulled a jar of instant coffee from the cupboard and grabbed my favorite coffee mug, the one with a mule and the word "Hooah" on it. It'd been a gift from my old friend, Jax. What had happened to him, anyway? It'd been months since I'd talked to him.

"Hey, Callie?"

My answer was an absent grunt. It was too early for proper conversation.

"Shouldn't you be on your way to that Ronan guy's house?"

I glanced at the clock on the stove. Seven-thirty? Shit, I was not going to make it to Dublin in thirty minutes!

Sam grabbed the cup out of my hands. "I'll make the coffee. Go get dressed!"

I sprinted for the bedroom and cursed my alarm for not going off while I dragged out my best white button-up and a pair of dark dress pants. I didn't know what the dress code for this job was, but I was going to lean toward business casual and hope for the best. The shirt was wrinkled and had a small stain on the bottom hem. Tucking in the shirt hid the stain, and I'd just have to deal with the wrinkles. Hopefully, it didn't cost me the job.

Sam was waiting by the door when I came out, steaming travel mug of coffee in hand. They passed it to me and pulled open the door. "Break a leg!"

There were two ways to get from our loft to Dublin. It was a straight shot up 315, and three miles shorter, but traffic there was always heavier. The 270 loop might be faster since there were more lanes, but it'd be crowded, especially on a Monday morning. I opted to face the crowded loop with a lead foot. At least there'd be room to pass there.

There was a minor wreck at the I-70 interchange, but when wasn't there? Traffic was down to two lanes and crawled around the overturned tractor-trailer. Once I got past that, though, it was smooth driving all the way to my exit. My old car didn't have GPS, so I used my phone to direct me the last few steps of the way.

Dublin was one of the nicest suburbs of Columbus, and it was where all the doctors and local celebs lived. It wasn't a surprise he lived out there. Big egos needed big houses, I guess. It seemed like a lot to take care of to me, although he probably had people for that. As much as I liked to gripe about rich people, there was a part of me that wanted that life. If someone showed up at my door with a billion dollars and the deed to a mansion, I sure as hell wasn't going to turn them down.

Ronan's house was a sprawling two-story of sandy-colored brick. Matching stone turrets jutted from the sides, giving the house a medieval castle vibe. It was down a short drive behind a brick wall. The only way in was through a big gate. I stopped at the gate and hit the intercom to announce I was there.

An unfamiliar voice answered, "Yes?"

"My name's Callie Hart. I was told to be here."

"You're late, Miss Hart," said the stranger impatiently.

I glanced at the clock on my dash. It was only three minutes past eight. Did that count as late? "Traffic sucked," I answered. "Ronan's expecting me."

He didn't answer. For a long minute, I thought maybe they weren't going to let me in, but the gate buzzed and slowly slid aside. Relieved, I pulled up the driveway and parked in front of the house. It was bigger than it looked from the road. Nicer, too.

I smoothed my hands over my wrinkled shirt, swallowed my nerves, and walked up to knock on the door.

An older man with a thin face opened it a moment later. He was wearing a black suit. Maybe I'd misjudged the dress code. "Miss Hart?" It was his voice I'd heard on the intercom.

"That's me."

He scrutinized me through narrowed eyes, then pushed the door open wider for me to enter.

Walking into Ronan's house was like stepping into another world. Huge blue Oriental rugs covered the polished hardwood floor. Sleek, modern chairs were parked in seemingly random places, though they looked like they belonged exactly where they'd been put. There wasn't a speck of dust or dirt anywhere.

The man who'd opened the door cleared his throat. "Your coat, Miss?"

"Oh, right." I took the coat off and handed it to him. "Who are you?"

"You may call me Thomas. Master McCalister has been expecting you."

"Master?" *What kind of ego do you have to have to insist that your staff refers to you as "Master" instead of mister?*

Someone was playing the piano nearby. I leaned forward, trying to track the source. While I couldn't recall the name of the song, I was sure I'd heard it before.

"This way, please."

Thomas led me from the first room into another that looked almost exactly like it, except the second room had a swooping stairway that led up to an indoor balcony. I was sure the structure had a name, but I didn't know enough about architecture to know what to call it. A chandelier hung from the ceiling, with glass beads dancing in the light.

The piano cut off suddenly as we entered a third room —this one narrower, with a semi-circular wall. Daylight flooded in through huge open windows, bathing a whole orchestra of instruments in light. They'd been pushed to the side so people could walk through, but the room held everything from the tiniest flute I'd ever seen to a huge bass.

Ronan sat at the piano, his forehead creased as he angrily scratched something on the page in front of him.

"So you're not just a pretty face," I said. "Tell me you don't play all these."

Thomas cleared his throat and gave me a sour look. "Miss Callie Hart, sir."

Ronan finally looked up from the piano. "Thank you, Thomas. You can go."

The butler gave me one last warning look before sliding out of the room and closing the double doors behind him.

I frowned. "Who peed in his bran flakes? Or is he always like that?"

"He takes some getting used to." Ronan's eyes sparkled with a smile his face didn't show as he rose to extend a hand to me. "I'm glad you came. I was starting to think you wouldn't."

I shook his hand the way I'd been taught in my job interview classes. A good, firm handshake was supposed to be the best introduction. "To be honest with you, I almost didn't. Working for you seems like it might be kind of dangerous."

"Would you believe me if I said it isn't usually?"

"Probably not." I glanced at the piano. The last time I'd seen one of those must've been while I was deployed. There was a music school in the village where we were stationed, and you could tell time by the different songs being played. The more complex the song, the later in the day it was.

"Do you play?" he asked, pulling me out of the memory.

"Only *Chopsticks*. Afraid I'm not all that musically inclined."

"It helps me think. But we can go elsewhere. Walter, the last head of security, didn't like being in here either."

I realized he was frowning, and I was holding myself stiffly. I must've looked uncomfortable as hell. "No, it's not that. I don't care. It's just… Well, this is awkward. I haven't been to a job interview in a long time. My friend got me the job at Kloud9, and before that, I was in Iraq."

"Then don't think of it as a job interview, at least not in the traditional sense." He gestured to an empty chair and pulled another one over. "Most job interviews are pointless, you know. By the time you've shown up, the employer has already done all the research they need and made up their mind."

"And have you? Made up your mind about me?"

Ronan smiled and crossed his arms. "Why Kloud9?"

His question surprised me. I'd been expecting an answer, or at least a non-answer, not another question. "Excuse me?"

"You've got an exemplary record as far as I can tell. You're more than capable with a gun. You made some very good shots last night. You reacted quickly to a potentially dangerous situation and saved lives. Even when you misjudged what you were up against, you were able to act under pressure. I'm sure some of that is thanks to your military background, but not everyone could do what you did." He leaned forward. "You know you are worth more than that place was paying you. So why work there?"

I shrugged. "What else should I be doing?"

He sighed and sat back, his expression disappointed. I hadn't given him the answer he was hoping for.

I need to recover. "When I came back, work was scarce," I continued. "I could've taken a job in a factory, I suppose. I know they pay more, but I didn't want to stand on a line every day doing mindless work. I want to help people. To matter."

Ronan nodded slowly. "I understand that. But with your training, you'd be a great candidate for a more traditional line of work. You might make an excellent police officer, for example. Why security and not the police academy?"

I considered the question carefully. A lot of former military went into law enforcement, but it wasn't for me. "Too much red tape. I knew there would be situations where I'd want to intervene, but all the rules and regulations would keep me from being able to do anything. The idea of walking away from someone I could've helped doesn't sit well with me."

"Now, that I believe. The position I want to offer you has *some* rules, but for the most part, I'd leave things to your judgment. I need someone who won't wait for permission to act if the situation calls for it, but who also knows when to back off. I won't lie to you. Most days will probably be boring, but if last night proves anything, it's that I need someone capable at my side. You proved you can handle yourself, even when going up against something...unusual."

"Some*thing*?" I repeated. "Not someone? What was that guy?"

He crossed one leg over the other and folded his fingers over his knee, staring at me in silence.

"No offense, Ronan, but if you can't tell me what the threats are, how can you expect me to take the job?" I stood. "Thanks for the offer, but I'm not sure it's for me."

He waited until I was halfway to the door before saying, "The creature that attacked me last night was a vampire, and I have every reason to believe he won't be the last to try. My life is in danger, Callie. So is yours."

CHAPTER FIVE

I wouldn't have believed him if he hadn't said it with a straight face. Vampires? Was this guy for real? Then again, I'd seen the attacker grow fangs and move supernaturally fast. He'd also turned to dust when I drove an oversized stick into his chest. Those things fit vampires, as far as I knew.

That didn't mean I had to buy his story. I folded my arms and stayed where I was. "Let me get this straight. You want me not only to believe vampires are real but that for some reason, they're out to get you? You do realize you sound like a paranoid weirdo? Why are they trying to kill you?"

"You saw him." Ronan avoided the question and rose to his feet. "And it's not just vampires. There are other things. Whatever they are, I'm confident you can handle them."

I shook my head. "I really don't think—"

"This isn't the first time you've encountered them, is it? You saw them before in Iraq."

My jaw snapped shut. How could he know about that?

Not only had I been told not to speak of it, but every mention of the incident had been wiped out of the records. My dead squadmates had been officially listed as missing in action.

Ronan walked to a small shelf near the piano and pulled a file out from under some books. He held it up so I could see it. "I read your account. I know what you saw. I know you believe me, even if you don't want to. You came here for answers, Callie. You can't ignore the answer because you don't like it."

"You're not supposed to know about that. You *can't* know that. The records were all destroyed." I clenched my fists to keep my hands from shaking.

"Not all the records. I have ways of finding information when I want it." He opened the file, reading from a document inside. "The perpetrator was bipedal and moved faster than I was able to perceive. I heard Private Jensen call out, then a burst of gunfire. By the time I arrived, he was bleeding out. I attempted to apply first aid in the field, but was unsuccessful."

"That's my personal statement." I stormed across the room and tried to take the folder from him.

He held it out of reach. "You know there are more threats out there than idiots picking fights in parking lots, Callie. Come work for me. Do something that will make a difference." Ronan lowered the folder and held it out to me. "You don't have to decide now. There's a sheet in the front with my offer on it. I think you'll find it fair."

I opened the folder. True to his word, the top page contained a list of benefits that came with the position, including a staggeringly good healthcare plan. At the bottom of the page, he'd written a six-figure number. "That isn't a real salary. No bodyguard makes that much." I almost asked him what the catch was, but he'd already told me: I'd have to deal with vampires and who-knew-what-else that might be trying to kill him.

I closed the folder. "What if I decline?"

"I think you'd be stupid to walk away, but I won't stop you." Ronan put his hands in his pockets and shrugged. "The vampire you killed last night was part of a larger group. They'll be looking to avenge their fallen friend, Callie. You won't be safe until the threat against my life is dealt with. Not only that, but think about the closure you'd be able to offer the families of your fallen brothers-in-arms."

I shook my head. "I'm not allowed to tell anyone anything."

"You're missing my point. The military might've sealed those files and threatened you into silence, but I won't do that." He sighed and took a step back. "As I said, you don't have to decide today. Take the day. Think it over. Maybe re-read some of what's in that file.

"I will need an answer by this time tomorrow. I can't go for long without someone to watch my back. I believe you're the one to do it, but I can't force you." Ronan stepped around me and opened the door. "You have my card?"

I nodded.

"Good. Thomas will show you out."

My mind was racing during the walk to the front door. Ronan was offering me answers. Well, not just me, but answers for the families of my squadmates. Their faces flashed in front of my eyes. I tried to imagine what their families might be going through, and how difficult it was for them, not knowing. They still thought their loved ones were just missing, and were probably holding out hope for a safe return. If I told them their husbands, fathers, sons weren't coming home, would that help or hurt?

The chill of the November air snapped me out of it. I rushed to my dented wreck of a car and sat in the driver's seat. I turned the key, fully intending to get back on the highway and drive home. If I hurried, I could still catch Sam before they had class. Even Sam would be able to see that working for Ronan was a bad idea. My predecessor had been murdered by a vampire, and Ronan was certain there were more vampires after him. Not only that, but they'd be after me once they figured out I'd staked the last one.

I don't need Ronan's job to protect myself from vampires. What was he going to do for me that I couldn't do? How about a six-figure income? I sighed and flipped the folder in the passenger seat open for another look at the promised salary. It didn't feel real to have this opportunity in front of me. Part of me wanted to sign on just for the money. So what if there were vampires involved? I'd already fought one and lived. Hell, I'd already survived two vampire attacks, if you counted the one in Iraq.

Sam hasn't, I thought. If the vampires did decide to come after me, the loft was the first place they'd look. Sam might've been a lot of things, but they weren't a fighter. They weren't into guns or weapons or any form of self-defense. If a vampire broke into our place looking for me, that'd be it for them. I had to do something to protect Sam.

At the very least, we needed to upgrade the locks and invest in serious home security. We might even be better off moving somewhere else as soon as we could afford it, though they'd want to stay close to their school.

This wasn't just about me anymore. I had to protect my friend. Besides, Ronan was right; I was more than qualified for the job. And didn't I owe the families of my squadmates justice? Finding the answers didn't mean I had to share them, but they'd be there if someone ever came to me, wanting to know what happened.

Then there was the money. A six-figure salary was life-changing. Sure, maybe I could get another, less dangerous job that offered great money and good benefits, but Ronan would give me something I didn't think I could find anywhere else.

Okay, Callie, those are the pros. Now, what are the cons? Well, I might die, for starters. That was what had happened to the last guy in the position. Not only that, but I don't know the first thing about Ronan. He didn't seem like a bad person, and I trusted my gut when it came to people. If there was something off about him, I'd have sensed it.

Once I thought about it, there was only one reason not to take the job—it was dangerous. Since when had I ever turned down something because it might put me in harm's way? If anything, I had a history of seeking out dangerous work. Looking at the offer from that perspective, this was the perfect job for me.

I sighed and rested my head against the steering wheel. *Don't make me regret this, brain*, I thought, and got back out of the car.

CHAPTER SIX

Thomas answered the door when I knocked. "Back so soon, Miss Hart? Did you forget something?"

"I need to see Ronan again."

He stepped back and gestured for me to go back to the music room. Ronan was at the window by the bookshelf, absently flipping through a copy of *Great Expectations* by Dickens, as I could see by the title on the cover. Had I ever read that one? It might've been required in high school, but I didn't recall what it was about. It certainly didn't seem like the sort of thing real people kept in their libraries.

"The only people who read Dickens are high school teachers or masochists," I said from the doorway.

Ronan looked up from the book and snapped it closed with one hand, smirking. "How do you know I'm not the latter?"

"As much money as you're offering me, I can't say I care what you do in your free time. Unless it's a danger to your personal safety, that is."

"And here I thought I'd scared you off with my talk of assassination plots and vampires."

I grunted and crossed my arms. "Scare me? Please, I've been on the 70/71 interchange at rush hour on Thanksgiving weekend. You'll have to work a little harder if you want to scare me."

He slid the book back into place. "I might yet. So, should I get the employment paperwork for you?"

"First," I said, holding up a hand, "I have questions I need answered before I sign anything."

"Fire away."

"What hours are we talking about?"

He shrugged. "Full-time. Occasional overtime. You'll be in charge of the whole security team, so the hours are yours to delegate how you want."

"Travel?"

"I travel several times a week. All your expenses will be covered, and you'll be paid for travel time on the job."

"Where to?"

He smiled. "London, Milan, Barcelona, Paris, New York, Berlin… This time of year, I'm doing two photoshoots a week, as many as four a week in the summer."

I blinked. I'd been halfway around the world, but I hadn't expected to do a lot of traveling when I got back—not that I didn't want to. Who doesn't want to visit a new city every week? But that meant a lot of time on the road in unfamiliar places with people I didn't know very well. It would seem like being deployed all over again, without the drills. "That's…a lot of travel."

"Trust me when I say it gets old very quickly." Ronan shrugged. "Any other questions for me?"

"A few. There are vampires out there; we covered that much. Anything else I should be aware of?"

Ronan hesitated.

I sighed and folded my arms over my chest. "You want me to protect you, I need to know everything. I can't protect you effectively if I don't know what I'm up against. Now, what else out there in the wild world wants to kill you, Ronan?"

"Nothing, I hope." He frowned and went to sit in the chair he'd occupied earlier, hands folded. "But there are other non-humans in the world. Other powers that you'll have to be briefed on to do your job effectively. For security reasons, however, I can't divulge that information until after you've signed the papers in your employment packet."

I supposed that was fair enough. The employment paperwork probably included a non-disclosure agreement that would prevent me from talking to the media about his life and what I saw, but would likely also ensure I couldn't tell Sam. Venting to Sam about work was part of my daily ritual. Once I signed on with Ronan, I'd have to be careful about what I let slip.

"What about your promise earlier? That I wouldn't be bound to secrecy concerning the vampires trying to kill you?"

"I stand by that," Ronan said, nodding. "No one should have to wonder what's happened to their loved ones, whether they're alive or dead. Still, I would think very carefully about the information you choose to tell outsiders. It was hard enough for you to learn about vampires, and you saw two of them with your own eyes. Hell, you killed one. The more people learn about the hidden world, the more dangerous their lives become. But I leave that up to you."

I considered what he said. I was only in contact with a few families from my former unit, and even then, we only emailed a few times a year. There were ways I could help them find closure without telling them everything. Given the edict from the higher-ups that I keep my mouth shut about the whole ordeal, I'd have to be careful. Everything I told someone else might make them a target.

"One more important question." I gripped the back of the chair I'd been sitting in earlier and studied his face, watching for any sign his next answer might be a lie. "How did you know what happened to my old unit in Iraq?"

"I told you. I have connections."

"They must be pretty high-level connections if they knew about that." I slid around the side of the chair and sat in it, leaning forward. "So, who is it? Someone in the CIA? FBI? Homeland? That's the only way you'd be able to pull those strings."

"Why does it matter so much to you how I know what I know?"

"Because if you're calling in favors with people in the alphabet agencies, that makes you a potential political target. We need to be concerned about more than just supernatural threats, Ronan. You're human, which means a bullet can kill you as easily as a vampire can. For all you know, there could be a sniper perched outside, peering through your window right now. Threats are all around you, and the more enemies you have, the more potential threats there are."

The corner of his mouth turned up. "See, right there is

why you're good at this. You don't trust anyone, do you, Callie? Not even me."

"For good reason. You won't even answer a simple question. Do you have government clearance, or don't you?"

"Yes," he answered smugly. "Of course I do, although maybe not in the way you mean it. I have a certain political value, but I don't expect foreign terrorists to take a swing at me. I'm far below their radar."

His answers weren't making sense, and he wasn't willing to give me more until I signed on. Nothing he'd said so far had changed my mind. All our conversation had done so far was cement in my mind that Ronan had secrets, and working for him was going to be a hazard to my health. Good, I thought. No job worth doing is going to be safe. What was the point in living if you didn't take a risk now and again?

A cellphone dinged somewhere in the room. "Excuse me." Ronan got up and retrieved his phone from where he'd left it on the piano, absently moving his thumbs over the screen. He frowned at whatever notification he'd just received. "I'm afraid I'm going to need an answer sooner rather than later, Callie."

"Another applicant for the position?"

"Not exactly. My family has just heard about what happened last night. If I don't have someone signed on to the position by the end of the day, my mother is threatening to come stay with me." He sighed. "I'd rather avoid that. If you're willing and can start tomorrow, I'd be happy to pay you a sign-on bonus to avoid it."

"You must not like your mother very much."

"When you meet her, you'll understand," Ronan said dryly and put the phone back down to pick up a stack of papers lying on the piano bench. He placed them on top of the instrument and clicked a pen. "So, do we have an agreement?"

"Say I take the job and decide it's not for me. Then what?"

Ronan lowered the pen, his frown deepening. "Then you walk away. No obligation to either party. It's all in the paperwork. I'll be disappointed, but I'll get over it. After what happened last night, you'll never work in security again without a strong recommendation. EEG is going to let you go, and that's the sort of black mark that will be difficult to get rid of. The world of corporate security cares more about following rules and pinching pennies than protecting people. They don't deserve someone as talented as you."

"And you do?"

"It's not about what I deserve. *You* deserve better. I hire the best. It's just business."

He was right. After all the training I'd had, everything I'd seen and been through, I was more experienced than half the staff at EEG put together. I'd only taken the job there to tide me over until something better came along, and here it was, staring me in the face. This was my "something better."

I pushed up from the chair and took the pen from him. "How much of an advance?"

Ronan's frown flipped back into one of his confident smirks. "I'm open to negotiations."

"You must really not want your mom crashing your

space." I signed next to the big X and initialed a few more pages.

After filling out all the other boring paperwork, I clicked the pen closed and flexed my aching hand. He hadn't been kidding when he'd said it was a whole packet of paperwork.

Ronan offered me his hand. "Welcome to the team, Callie."

CHAPTER SEVEN

S am was waiting for me when I came through the door, sipping tea from a coffee cup. They'd put on a baggy OSU shirt and a pair of sweatpants. Guess Sam had decided to skip class, not that it'd hurt their grades any. They were a straight-A student with a big art scholarship.

"So?" Sam asked, eyes big. "Did you get the job?"

I decided to let them sweat it for a minute and went straight to the fridge in search of something that wasn't coffee or beer to drink. We still had a few sodas in the back.

"Callie, come on! I'm dying here. Did you get it, or didn't you?"

I popped the top and chugged down half the soda before turning around with a big grin. "Of course I did."

Sam screeched with joy and put aside their cup to hug me. "I knew it! Tell me more! How much does it pay? What was his house like? Does he have a dog? He looked like a dog person. God, I wish we could get a dog."

I produced the folder from inside my coat and showed them the page with the salary information. Sam's eyes practically bulged out of their head.

"And he gave me a sign-on bonus." I waved the check in front of her. "What do you say we cash it and go celebrate?"

Sam grabbed the check and made a face. "Damn. What the hell am I doing in college? I should drop out and go into security."

I pulled the check away from them and stuck my tongue out. "Yeah, right. I can see you on your first day. You'd be falling all over yourself, going gaga over the paintings on the wall. He had a ton of them. Real artsy type guy. You'd like him."

"You can tell me all about it over lunch." Sam hopped excitedly up and down before skipping toward their room. "And we're going shopping at Easton to get you some new clothes, girl! Be ready in ten!"

I frowned down at my wrinkled blouse. "What's wrong with my clothes?"

Sam didn't answer. They were too busy throwing on clothes of their own. I sighed and trudged back to the bedroom to change.

Sam and I hit the shops hard and had most of Ronan's sign-on bonus spent by two in the afternoon. I hadn't been clothes-shopping in over a year, and Sam insisted that I buy designer threads. "You're working for a fashion model," they'd said, piling my arms high with dresses and skirts. "You've got to look the part!"

I shifted the pile as they dropped a pair of bright red heels on it. "I have to dress for functionality, Sam. I'm going to be on my feet all day. Not to mention, I have to be able to carry a gun."

"You can get one of those sexy thigh holsters. Or, what about those tiny one-shot pistols the Old West saloon girls used to carry in their corsets?"

With a grunt, I dropped the pile onto a bench outside the fitting room area and shook out my arms, which had gone numb under the weight. "I don't think they even make derringers anymore." I remembered the vampire from last night. No matter how many bullets I'd put in him, he hadn't stopped coming. "Besides, sometimes you need more than one shot to take down the bad guys."

"Just go try some stuff on, would you?" Sam shoved me toward one of the fitting rooms. "We're burning daylight, and we haven't even gotten to the best part of the day: the afterparty!"

In the end, I settled on a couple of nice white shirts and blazers in a few different colors and styles. Sam didn't approve of my choices and talked me into trading out a few pairs of dress pants for skirts. It took some doing, but I finally talked them out of anything bright or striped with rainbow colors. In addition to the work clothes I bought, I added a single dress, but only because I didn't own anything nice enough to go out in. I wanted the black one, but Sam swapped it out at the last minute for the light blue version, saying it was my color.

After shopping, I was exhausted, but Sam wanted to go out. It'd been a long time since I'd done anything for fun, especially dancing and drinking, so I decided to indulge them. I put on the blue dress, did my hair, and even put on a little makeup.

Next thing I knew, we were seated at a table in the wings of a crowded dance club with flashing lights all around, and I was passing a beer to Sam. Upbeat pop music pounded in my ears—not my first choice in music, but at least it wasn't country.

Sam bounced in their seat. Rather than put on a dress, Sam had chosen a rainbow-striped shirt and skinny jeans. I thought the sparkly silver blazer was a bit much, but it was getting them plenty of looks. Several people had stopped by our table to tell Sam they liked it, and they seemed happy with the attention. Typical Sam.

Sam grabbed my arm and flashed a big grin. "See, Callie? This isn't so bad, is it?"

I scanned the crowd and tried not to think about all the ways things could go wrong with so many people packed in that tight. Drunk people, loud music, crowds… It was a recipe for disaster in there.

"Hey." Sam grabbed my face with both hands and forced me to look at them. "You okay in there?"

"Yeah. Of course I am." I picked up the beer and drained it. "Why wouldn't I be? Having the time of my life."

"Well, you don't look like it. You look like someone stole your puppy. Come on, Callie! We're supposed to be celebrating."

"Right. I'm going to go get us some more drinks." As soon as I stood, the song ended and a familiar tune began, one I must've heard Sam play a thousand times in our apartment. I knew I was done for as soon as it came on.

Sam jumped to their feet, a big smile on their face. "Forget the beers! This is my song, Callie!" Sam grabbed me before I could get away and practically dragged me onto the dance floor. Their fingers slid out of mine, and they left me standing awkwardly in the middle of everyone.

"Sam," I shouted above the thumping music, "I don't know how to dance!"

"Of course you do. Everyone knows. You just *move.*" They did some kind of dance move that should've been impossible with functioning joints.

I cringed.

"Come on, girl. You can do it! Try!"

Against my better judgment, I did. Fit as I was, my knees did not like the odd movement, but I managed to convince them to do it. For the next four minutes, Sam continued to give me pointers. I almost had the hang of it when the song ended and another started. With the change in beat, it felt like I had to learn all over again. After a few more minutes, I was soaked in sweat, and certain I looked anything but sexy. There was a reason I became a soldier and not a ballerina.

As time ground on, I noticed three guys circling us. They weren't dancing or going to any particular destination, yet every time I looked up, they were in different locations, watching us with their creepy smiles. When I turned toward where I knew one of them was, I found him gone. Maybe he'd never been there, and I was imagining things.

You're being paranoid, I told myself. It was Ronan's fault. He'd gotten me all wound up, telling me that the vampires might be out to get me if they found out I'd killed one of them. I should've known better than to go out.

"Hey, you okay?" Sam grabbed my arm as the song changed to something slower.

"Yeah. I just need a drink is all. I think I'm going to sit this one out if you don't mind."

"Then I'll come with you."

"No," I said a little too quickly. "You should enjoy yourself. I'm very awkward out here. I'm more used to carrying heavy gear and shooting things than dancing."

Sam frowned. "Okay, if you're sure."

"I'm sure."

Navigating my way back to the table through all the other bodies was difficult. I was disoriented from dancing and the flashing lights, but I finally made it back and sat down with a huff, wincing as my feet reminded me I hadn't worn heels in far too long. I never should've let Sam talk me into them.

It wasn't long before Sam came running up to the table with two guys they'd met on the dance floor. They tossed the car keys to me and told me not to wait up. Again, typical Sam. Sometimes I envied their free spirit. I wouldn't feel sorry for them when they were hung over the next day, though. I owed Sam one for making me dance like an idiot.

"You sure you'll be okay?" they asked.

I flashed a confident grin. "Yeah, I'm fine. Go have fun."

"Okay, Callie." They leaned over to give me a hug.

I squeezed them back. "Be safe. Text me later to let me know you're okay."

"You too."

Sam and I parted ways. In a flash, the trio was gone and

I was alone at my table, wondering what to do with myself the rest of the night.

A waitress appeared and put a Bloody Mary on the table in front of me.

"Oh, I didn't order anything." I tried to hand it back to her.

She shook her head and pointed to a table one level up. "Gentleman in the suit paid for it. Said you'd know what it meant."

I followed her finger to where she'd pointed. A man sat at a table by himself, too well dressed to fit in with the rest of the club clientele. I'd never seen him before, but something about him sent a chill down my spine. Whoever he was, I wasn't going to let him get to me.

I thanked the server, picked up the drink, and climbed the stairs to put it on his table. "I think this was delivered to me by mistake."

"No mistake," he said and smiled.

That was when I saw the fangs. I guess it's only paranoia if you don't turn out to be right.

I picked up the drink and splashed the contents in his face. I don't care if you're a vampire, a human, or any other sentient being, a bloody Mary to the eyes *burns*. The vampire let out a pained growl and reached up to clear the drink from his eyes. I grabbed his chair and tipped it back, and he landed on his back with a loud thump. Then I dropped the glass on his chest. "Follow me, and you'll wind up like your friend, creep."

Everyone in the area was staring at me, and I spied Security heading my way. It was as good a time as any to call it a night, so I grabbed my purse and hurried toward the nearest exit.

The parking garage was strangely cold, even for November in Ohio. I chalked it up to the dress since I wasn't used to wearing them. Still, I couldn't shake the feeling that something was wrong and picked up the pace. The sound of my heels clicking on the pavement echoed through the parking area, the only sound other than the buzz of the overhead lights.

I swept the area visually for threats, eyes darting from one parked car to another, but nothing seemed out of the ordinary. There was a white van parked near my car with a logo for a security company I'd never heard of, which seemed a little odd, but I was probably making something of nothing. It made sense that a club would have contracted security. If not the club, there were plenty of other buildings around that needed security overnight. Yeah, that had to be it.

My car waited at the end of the row. I'd nearly reached it when two men stepped out from behind the van, blocking my way. I stopped, turned, and almost walked right into two more. One of them was the guy I'd just dumped the bloody Mary on.

I opened my purse and pulled out my phone. "One more move and I call the police."

"You don't need them," the Bloody Mary vampire said, stepping forward. "You will come with us."

"Like hell, I will."

A fifth guy I hadn't seen rolled open the side door of the van.

The vampire grinned. "I'm afraid I'm going to have to

insist, Ms. Hart. It's for your own good." He grabbed my arm and yanked me toward the van.

What took place next happened on automatic. I tried to pull away and shouted for help, my brain racing in a panic. All I wanted was for him to stop. Something inside me screamed to life and lashed out in a bright arc of glowing power. It slammed into the vampire dragging me toward the van.

He let me go, looking at the back his hand in horror. "What the hell?"

Frost spread over his fingers, up the sides of his face, and over his hair. He tried to reach for me again, but he froze solid before he could close his fingers around me.

The others, who I assumed were also vampires, backed away, thinking better of attacking me while I stared at my hand. What had I done?

I didn't have time to process it before the boom of a gunshot rang through the parking garage and the vampire shattered into a thousand pieces like a glass dropped from a high rise. Tires squealed and a black SUV tore out of its parking spot, moving so fast it almost tipped over when it rounded the corner. The vampires yelped and ran to their van, pulling out after the other vehicle.

In the space of a few seconds, I was alone in the parking garage with the shattered remains of another dead vampire. What the hell had just happened? Had *I* frozen him? And who'd fired the shot that saved my ass?

Police sirens screamed nearby and jerked me back to the moment. I couldn't be caught standing over another destroyed body, not so soon after the incident at Kloud9. I needed to get out of there. Everything else I could deal with later.

I backed away from the vampire pieces on the ground—which were melting and turning to dust—rushed to my car, and unlocked it with shaky hands. I didn't pull out of the parking garage as quickly as the other two, but I'd be lying if I said I didn't get out of there as fast as I could.

CHAPTER EIGHT

My hands shook as I gripped the steering wheel. I didn't even remember driving back to the loft, but there I was, parked in my designated space. The windshield had fogged from my breath. How long had I been sitting there in the cold?

I just kept going back over the incident in my mind, playing the scene in slow motion as if I could find some hole in the logic of it. It couldn't be real. People didn't just freeze solid. Then again, he hadn't exactly been a person. He was a vampire. Still, *I* had done that. Whatever power had snapped out and washed over him, turning him into a block of ice, it had come out of me.

I pried my fingers off the steering wheel and stared at them, trembling in the cold. They looked like normal fingers, normal hands. Where the hell had that come from?

Then there was the shooter. I was sure I'd heard a gunshot. The shot had hit the vampire, shattering him like glass. Or had it just been his head that had shattered? I was getting the details mixed up. My head was swimming from the stress, the drinks, and the loud music. How much had I imagined, and how much was real? Maybe none of it was.

Get it together, Callie. I blew out a deep breath and counted to three. *Whatever happened, sitting out here in the cold isn't going to change it. You're not safe here.* My eyes snapped open. I had to get somewhere safe behind locked doors. Shit, maybe I should call Sam and warn them. If the vampires were at the club, they saw us together. Sam could be in danger too.

I threw open the car door and stepped out, scanning the dark parking lot. A single streetlight leaned over the back lot, not quite bright enough to illuminate everything. There were plenty of corners and deep shadows where a vampire could hide. I tried to ignore them as I hurried to the door.

My pace didn't slow until I'd reached the loft and slipped inside, slamming the door closed behind me. I made sure to lock the door, then went around checking all the windows, even the ones in Sam's room. They wouldn't mind. Once I was sure all the entrances were secure, I checked them one more time, just in case. This was one of those times I wished I still carried a gun.

Now what? I stared at the deadbolt. Could a vampire break down a deadbolted door? Probably. *Maybe it's like in the movies and they need permission to enter.* I hoped that was true, but hoping it didn't make me feel any safer.

Sam! I remembered suddenly and pulled out my phone, but stopped just short of dialing them. What would I say if they picked up? *Hey, Sam, sorry to interrupt your threesome, but I just froze a vampire, then some weirdo shot him. Wanted you to watch out, you know, just in case.*

I sighed and lowered the phone. Sam was open-minded when it came to just about everything, but vampires, assassins, and magic—or whatever I'd done in the parking garage—were out of their wheelhouse. They wouldn't know what to do with that information. Sam was a great friend, but there were things even they couldn't deal with. I was on my own.

Not knowing what else to do, I took a shower, standing under the faucet until the water ran cold. I spent the whole time stuck in the moment again, going back over it and analyzing every detail. There had to be a rational explanation for what'd happened. It was one thing for there to be vampires in the world. Hell, maybe there were werewolves and little Tinkerbell fairies too. But magic? You'd think I'd know if I had magic powers.

I wrapped a towel around myself and stood in front of the cloudy mirror for a moment before wiping my wrist across it. The face staring back at me didn't look like it belonged to the sort of girl who got caught up in those things. My life was boring. Average grades in school, average family, normal job. The only thing that had ever been different about me was how normal I was.

Okay, if I did it once, I could do it again. I turned on the faucet and focused on the water running down the drain. In my mind, I tried to recreate the panicked feeling from the parking garage, but I couldn't call it back up. I was unsettled as hell after what'd happened, but the fear had fled. All I felt now was frustration. Why was all of this happening to me? Why had I asked to be transferred to the night shift at Kloud9? Had I really been so desperate for one more dollar an hour? And why the fuck couldn't I freeze the water running down the drain?

I shut the water off with a sigh. This was crazy. What was I getting involved with? At least I didn't have to worry about money for a while.

I dressed in my favorite pair of pajamas and checked the locks again. Sam had texted me a picture of them in a dark movie theater, sitting beside one of the guys they'd left the club with. The caption promised Sam would be back in time for class in the morning, but I wasn't holding my breath. When they were like this, they usually skipped class a few days in a row until they got it out of their system.

Rather than go to sleep, I sat in my bed, scrolling through social media feeds. Everyone I knew was posting photos of mundane things. It was hard to believe none of them knew what I knew—that there were vampires lurking in the city, and maybe worse things.

One of the big exposed pipes in the ceiling rattled, and I almost jumped out of my skin. Dammit, calm down. That was just the heat kicking on. Just the same, I got up to close and lock my bedroom door, only to stop once I'd grabbed the doorknob. I'd feel a lot safer with a weapon.

I knew it was silly, but security was mostly an illusion anyway. Locked doors and windows might make people feel safe, but a determined thief could get past them easily. A vampire could do it without breaking a sweat.

I stalked into the kitchen, determined to find some-thing—anything—that would help me defend myself against a vampire if one broke into my room. The gun EEG had issued had to be left at work, and I'd turned it in when they'd suspended me. I hoped Ronan would issue me a new one. Until then, a steak knife would have to do.

This is dull as fuck, I thought, lifting the knife into the light. *It couldn't stab a tater tot, let alone a vampire. Guess I should fix that.* For the next fifteen minutes, I sat at the kitchen table, sharpening all our knives. Just in case.

The entire time, I held the image of that Bloody Mary vampire in my mind. He was gone, but his friends were still out there, and if they came through my door, or after me and mine, they were going to be in a world of hurt.

Knives sharpened, I selected the biggest one, went back to my room, and locked the door. With the knife tucked under my pillow and my blanket pulled up to my chin, I fell asleep, dreaming of a world without vampires.

CHAPTER NINE

To make up for being late the day before, I showed up for work early. When I arrived, Ronan was in his music room again, only this time he was playing the violin. I've never been one for music, but if I had to choose between the piano and the violin, I'd say he was much better at the violin. Maybe not at playing; I didn't know enough about either instrument to tell anyone what was technically good or not. There was just something different about his face when I walked in and found him playing that day as opposed to the day before, the sort of passionate expression people only reveal when they truly care about their art.

Thomas left me in the doorway, where I stood waiting for him to finish. He had his back to me, which meant he didn't notice me for a while. After a few minutes, I got bored with standing there and went to pick a book up from where it rested on the arm of a chair. It was the copy of *Great Expectations* he'd been leafing through the day before. I tried to flip it over without losing his spot, but the book slipped out of my hands and fell to the floor with a bang.

Ronan's bow screeched and he spun around.

I cringed. "Sorry."

His face lit up with a boyish smile. He placed his violin carefully back on the stand. "Callie! Thomas should've told me you were here. Let me guess—he just shoved you into the room and shut the door behind you? Sounds like him. You didn't have to stand there. Why didn't you stop me?"

"It seemed rude to interrupt. You were pretty into it."

"I must've been if I didn't hear you come in. Sorry. I promise I don't spend all my time in here. It's just that playing keeps my mind too busy to think about anything else. Otherwise, I'd be a mess."

It was hard to imagine someone so put together being a mess. He probably had a whole team of people who picked out his clothes, did his hair, and maybe even polished his shoes. Based on the salary he'd promised me and the house, Ronan had to be obscenely rich.

He walked up to me, beaming from ear to ear. "You've got new shoes."

I looked down at my feet. Everything I had on was new, but he'd noticed the shoes? "Uh, yeah."

"You can tell a lot about a person by the shoes they choose to wear." Ronan grabbed both doors and threw them open, gesturing for me to follow. "It's one of those details people often overlook, but it's the details that make the person, Callie."

He led me down a different hallway with pictures on the wall, all modern art pieces that Sam would've loved. I didn't get them. The walls, however, were pristine white, the baseboards free of dust.

The hallway spilled into a dining area with a long table. Three brass light fixtures with swirling designs hung over it, but they were off. The only light came from the gray morning outside, filtering in through three large picture windows. The pool in the backyard had been covered for the year, but the cover on it was clean enough to eat on.

"This way," Ronan called.

I turned away from admiring the backyard and found him waving to me from another doorway. "I'm going to get lost in this place."

"There's a map in your orientation paperwork. You'll have plenty of time to go over that on the plane."

"Plane?" I stepped through a stone arch into a kitchen a five-star chef would've killed for. There were two islands: one for the sink, and the other an L-shaped bar complete with bar stools. The countertops must've been real marble. Someone like Ronan wouldn't bother with knock-offs. Everything was made of dark wood, stainless steel, or patterned glass.

Ronan went straight to the fridge. "Did you have break-fast? There's fruit in the basket there, or I can call Jeanie in to make you something. I'm not much of a cook, but she's amazing." He pulled out a plastic container full of thick green liquid and gulped some of it down.

I cringed and lost what little appetite I had at the sight of it. "I can tell. What is that?"

He lowered the container and studied it as he wasn't sure. "Something with kale probably. I'm on a strict diet until all these stupid underwear shoots are done. After this,

I'm NPO for six hours. I'll be practically dehydrated by the time we get to the shoot."

"NPO?"

"Nothing passed orally. No food. No drink." He shook his head. "I don't recommend it, but there's a price for making your living by looking like this." Ronan took another sip from the bottle and lowered it. "Dammit, that came out wrong. I promise I'm only about fifty percent stuck-up male model. One second." He pulled out his phone, took a selfie, and turned all his attention to posting it somewhere online.

I folded my arms. More hashtag than heartthrob was right. "Yeah, I can see that."

"This is part of my job. I can't get gigs if I'm not constantly posting, Callie. Oh, that reminds me!" He darted to the other side of the kitchen to retrieve a white plastic bag from the counter that he held out to me. "This is for you. Part one of your welcome package."

I took the bag and peeked inside, frowning. "A phone?"

"I'm sure you have one already. Everyone has a cell phone. But since you're running my security now, you need to have a top-of-the-line model. You'll be monitoring online threats as well as those to my person, which means you need to have a fully capable phone. Not only that, but this one will integrate with the house security like mine does. You'll be able to control everything from the thermostat to the gate remotely. Whether we're in Berlin or you're sitting at home, you can shut everything down at a moment's notice."

"Cool." I took the phone out of the bag and turned the box over. He wasn't kidding when he said it was a top-of-the-line model. Was this one available publicly yet? How did he get it?

"Right. Let's get you everything else you need. Oh, and I should show you the panic room."

Panic room? I raised an eyebrow, but that was all I had time to do because Ronan was already scurrying to the next room. I practically had to jog to catch up. "You said something about a plane earlier?"

He nodded as we reached a narrow stairway hidden in a little alcove. "I have a photoshoot in New York this afternoon, so I won't be able to give you the full tour of the house. We'll be back late. I hope that's not a problem? I did tell you about the hours?"

"You did," I huffed. I was in good shape, but Ronan was taking the stairs two at a time at a crazy pace. Damn Sam for insisting I wear even these low heels instead of flats, on the premise that my employer was a model and I couldn't look frumpy. "It's not a problem."

At the top of the stairs, Ronan made a sharp right and darted into a room the size of a small bedroom. It had been transformed into a security station, with monitors on one wall. They boasted a good-quality color image, not the fuzzy black and white of the factory cameras. Next to the monitors was a sleek desktop computer, and next to that, a huge gun safe.

Ronan grabbed a yellow sticky note from beside the computer and typed in the code to open the safe. "I know you know your way around firearms. Walter wasn't bad with them. He liked big guns, though, and I kept telling him we didn't need that sort of protection."

The gun safe was full of...well, guns—more guns than

I'd seen since I left the service. There were enough there to equip a private army, although the hiring materials Ronan had given me stated I only had a security staff of two other part-timers.

"Maybe you should've listened to Walter." I picked out a Remington 12-gauge pump-action shotgun and looked down the barrel. "Good model. Nice sights. Some of the best stopping power available to civilians."

"Civilians." Ronan chuckled. "I like it."

"Good for close-range encounters if you've got only one intruder." I put the shotgun back and picked up an AR-15. "Now, this almost feels familiar."

"I imagine you carried something similar in the military?"

I checked the rifle over. "Sort of. The civvy version has a longer barrel, but the trigger assembly is the same, and they handle similarly. Iron sights, huh?" I frowned and pushed open the safe door a little more. There were some optics there, but none of them were compatible with the AR-15. It wasn't useless without a decent scope, but the three-round burst fire was much more effective when you could see what you were aiming at.

"Something wrong?" Ronan leaned over the gun safe's door.

"Not wrong. It would be better with more accessories."

"Everything's better with accessories," Ronan agreed. "Make a list of what you want, and I'll make sure you get it."

I'd already put the rifle back and turned to the other door to examine the handguns. "This is my favorite," I said, pulling out a Colt .45 M1911. "Lightweight. Reliable. Easy to conceal. Lots of customization options." I lowered the gun. "What about body armor?"

Ronan gestured for me to follow him to a metal locker on the other side of the room. He unlocked that one with a key that he tossed to me afterward. Inside were three ballistic vests, thin enough in profile to fit under an over-shirt. I pushed them aside and eyed an over-the-clothes version with tactical pockets. "Was Walter wearing one of these when...when it happened?"

"Unfortunately, short of riot gear, I'm not sure there is any type of body armor that can stop vampire fangs."

"They make Kevlar sleeves for your neck," I said, pushing them all aside. "These are great, but they're all designed to fit a male frame. They'll be long on me and fit wrong in the arms. We'll have to upgrade that."

"Noted." He rubbed the back of his head. "Actually, it might be easier if you got a catalog or something and just put the order in. I'll pay for whatever upgrades are needed, of course. Maybe if Walter'd had the sort of experience you do, we could've been better prepared."

I turned away from the armor. "I'm sorry. Were you close?"

He shrugged. "It's hard not to be when you're with someone day in and day out. Walter, though? He was always...distant. Very professional. Very good at his job. Just the sort of person Mother would hire." He sighed and pushed off the safe to slap a panel in the wall. It rolled aside to reveal a big red button. "You, though? She'd hate every-thing about you."

I put the gun back, closed the safe, and gestured to the button. "What's that?"

RENÉE JAGGÉR

"Panic button." He patted the clear plastic covering over it. "Hit this baby, and it'll drop ballistic shutters around the core section of the house. That includes this room, my master suite, and the guest room. An alert will automatically be sent to both our phones, the police and fire departments, and to my mother."

"Your mother?"

"Her idea. Anyway..." He pointed up. "If it gets hit a second time, there's an escape hatch in the ceiling in here. Ladder drops down, and you can get into the attic crawl space. There are enough supplies up there at any given time to keep two people alive for three days. There's a company that comes in and replenishes all that for me once a month overnight. I'll give you their schedule. You'll have to stay in the house when they're here. I don't like outside guests to be left unsupervised."

I frowned at the panel. If he hadn't pointed it out, I would've missed it. "No offense, Ronan, but don't you think all this is a little much? I mean, you're just a model."

"And you're just a security guard." He crossed his arms. "Except you're not. No one is just whatever their job is."

"I'm sorry. I didn't mean—"

His face broke into a smile. "I'm messing with you. Don't worry about it. I promise you're not the first person to assume I am just a rich pretty boy. You won't be the last. Sometimes, though, it's better to let people believe that story. You'd be surprised by how far that gets me half the time." He clapped his hands. "Now, you'd better pick out your gun. I want you armed whenever you're with me."

I grabbed the Colt from the gun safe, along with a belt holster and a couple of magazines, and followed Ronan through the rest of the upstairs as he pointed out different rooms. In addition to the bedrooms, security room, kitchen, dining room, and music room, the house had a library that spanned both floors tucked into one of the far corners. The library was the first room we came to where not everything was spotless. Books lay in random piles near chairs or sat dog-eared on the window seat. It wasn't the largest private library, but he easily had more books than I'd read in my entire life.

"I don't come in here as much as I used to," he said, gripping the edge of one of the ornate bookshelves.

"You just read *Great Expectations* over and over, then?" I scanned the shelves and found them full of classics like Austen, Twain, Hemmingway, and Tolstoy. Then on the next shelf, he had collectors' editions of several famous fantasy novels.

Ronan shrugged. "Not really. I'm bored with most of these books. If I'm honest, even my music felt stale until this morning. I'm not sure what changed. I just woke up and felt...better. But you don't want to hear about all that." He waved a hand, dismissing the conversation. "We've got a plane to catch in a few hours, and you have things to read."

Ronan collected a whole box of spiral-bound books from the library table and held them out to me.

I reached to pick up the first book in the box, only to find it was all one big book. "*The Art of Security* by Walter Wyman? This thing must weigh fifty pounds!"

"What can I say? Walter was thorough. He wanted to make sure his replacement was well-prepared." He hefted the box into my arms and checked his watch. "You'll have plenty of time to read it on the plane. The driver should be here any minute, and I haven't finished my smoothie. I'll call for you when he gets here?"

"Yeah, sure." With a grunt, I lowered the box to the ground and scowled at it. Being Ronan's bodyguard wasn't supposed to have homework. The flight from Columbus to New York wasn't going to be near long enough for me to make it through that entire book. "And here I thought Dickens would make for dry reading," I grumbled and opened the book.

CHAPTER TEN

R onan introduced me to his driver. It was a thirty-minute drive to the airport beyond the outer belt. That sounded like it would be enough time for me to start going through the book Ronan had handed me, but I decided the time would be better spent getting the new phone set up.

As soon as I got it working, I found he'd already shared his schedule with me and given me more to read in my email. I groaned inwardly. There was enough reading material to keep me busy for weeks. Unlike Ronan, I wasn't a bibliophile. I read a few books here and there, but it wasn't something I'd go out of my way to do.

When I looked up, we were at the airport, or rather, *an* airport. There were planes taking off and coming in over our heads, but we hadn't gone to any of the public termi-nals. Instead, the driver had driven us to the edge of some tarmac, near which an unmarked jet waited. *Of course he would have his own private jet.*

I slid the new phone into my pocket and frowned out

the window. We weren't alone on the tarmac. Two vans were parked between where our car had stopped and the plane. Standing in front of one of those vans were a tall, bald man in an expensive suit, but he wasn't my concern. I was more worried about the paramilitary types standing around him. "Military contractor" was the nice way of saying mercenary, also known as assholes who did half the work and got twice the pay of real soldiers. We'd had a few on the base while I was stationed in Iraq, but I'd always done my best to avoid them. They didn't associate with grunts like me anyway. What were they doing waiting for us on the tarmac, though?

My heart fluttered in a panic for a moment. What if they'd been sent by someone higher up in the government to remind me to keep my mouth shut? Maybe what'd happened a few nights ago at Kloud9 had finally gotten up the chain, and they wanted to make sure I was still behaving myself.

No, they wouldn't send a bunch of mercs to do that kind of dirty work. That wasn't how the feds did things. They knew better than to try to intimidate a former soldier with guns and muscle. If I was going to be threatened by someone high up, I figured it would come in the form of an official letter, an anonymous phone call, or frozen assets. Those guys were here for something else.

Ronan narrowed his eyes and frowned when he saw them.

I grabbed for the door, intending to get out and handle the situation. I was responsible for his personal safety now, after all.

"Wait here," Ronan said. "I'll deal with them."

"No offense, Ronan, but you shouldn't go out there alone. Those men are armed, and we don't know what they want. It would be safer if you stayed in the vehicle and let me find out what they want first."

He laughed as if I were being paranoid. "I know them, and I know why they're here. I'm not in any danger with them, I promise you."

Before I could stop him, he was out the door, straightening the collar of his coat and strolling over to meet with them. Rather than wait in the car as he'd instructed, I got out to follow. Ronan might be my boss, but I wasn't going to let him win every argument, especially when it came to letting me do my job.

The bald man met Ronan with a handshake. "Good to see you're well, Ronan."

"It's been a while, Vaughn. How's your arm? Last time I saw you, it was in a sling."

"Never better." He demonstrated by making a fist and flexing his fingers. Vaughn's eyes shifted to me. "This must be your new head of security."

Ronan turned as if to introduce me, but I stepped in and held out my hand. "Callie Hart."

"I hope you've got a strong personality, Ms. Hart," Vaughn said, taking my hand. "You'll need it to work with this one. He's a stubborn boy."

"I'd rather be stubborn than ugly and bald," Ronan quipped.

Vaughn laughed and ran a hand over his smooth head. "Yes, well, we all have our gifts. Some of us look good in photographs. Others help dictate the rise and fall of dynasties."

Their back-and-forth seemed good-natured on the surface, but underneath, there was a tense thread. Whatever their history, Vaughn and Ronan didn't like each other.

I scanned the faces of the mercs at Vaughn's back but didn't find anyone I recognized. None of them stood out or even twitched. They were as still as the mannequins at the factory. The logo on the vans behind them, however, was familiar. I'd seen one exactly like it in the parking garage the night before.

"You're with Meyer Securities?" I asked Vaughn.

He chuckled. "Young lady, I *am* Meyer Securities. I own the company. It's the largest private security contractor in the United States, I should add."

Ronan shook his head. "You can stop trying to sell it to her. I pay her enough so she's not interested."

Vaughn folded his hands behind his back and squared his shoulders. "It's not always about the money. Personal security has its advantages. Safer. Local. A nice, comfortable job. If ever you start to feel like you don't belong over here, Ms. Hart, Meyer Securities has people stationed in thirty countries around the world. We rebuild governments and fight terrorists. If you're interested in Fashion Week, I think you'll be more comfortable with Ronan."

I glanced at Ronan, trying to read his expression. He was focused wholly on Vaughn, but he looked like he wanted to be anywhere but here.

"Thanks, Vaughn," I said, "but I did my time with Uncle Sam. I'm good."

Ronan's shoulders relaxed as soon as I turned Vaughn

down. Had he really been worried that I'd take the man up on the offer? "What do you really want?"

"I have correspondence from your mother." Vaughn opened his jacket.

On instinct, my hand drifted closer to the gun at my belt.

Vaughn paused when he saw her react and smirked before producing an envelope that he held out to Ronan.

Ronan took the envelope, tore it open, and scanned the handwritten letter inside. "Looks like you'll be joining us on our trip to New York."

"Why?" I didn't mean for the question to slip out like that. It was supposed to come out more tactful and less defensive. As it was, it sounded like I was jumping to defend my job as his bodyguard.

"We can talk about it on the plane." Ronan folded the letter and stuck it in his pocket. "If we don't get in the air in the next few minutes, we're going to miss our takeoff window. You'll be leaving your people here?"

"I'm in charge of security," I said, crossing my arms. "If you bring anyone, they'll have to coordinate with me."

Vaughn smiled and flashed me a quick glance. "Of course. I think you'll be more than enough protection for both of us, Ms. Hart." He gestured for his people to go.

They immediately turned and marched back to their vans.

I watched them climb in one by one. It couldn't be a coincidence that the same company's van had been parked outside the club last night. Had the vampires gotten into it to make their escape or just one that looked like it? I couldn't remember. After tossing and turning all night, the specifics of what had happened were skewed. When I checked the news in the morning, there weren't any reports of body parts found in any parking garages, so either he'd turned to dust before they got there or I'd dreamed the whole thing.

If it was real, Vaughn might be connected. The question was, how?

We boarded the plane, and I tried not to gawk at how nice everything was. I'd been on plenty of planes, and even jumped out of a few, but never a private jet. Unlike a normal airplane, there were only a handful of seats, each more like a padded armchair than how I pictured an airplane seat. Flawless white leather covered the seats, and polished wood panels ran the length of the cabin. Rather than all face forward, the seats had been arranged in quads so that when Ronan and I took our seats, we were facing each other. Vaughn sat in the second quad of seats but made sure to sit where he could keep smiling at me.

I didn't like him, and not just because he might be connected to the assholes who'd attacked me the night before. It wasn't even because he was the head of a bunch of glory-hunting mercs, although those two things didn't help. There was something about the smug way he talked down to both Ronan and me, as if he thought he was better than both of us put together.

My fingers dug into the plush armrests as the plane took off, and I tried to stare down his grinning face. Maybe he's just trying to be pleasant, I told myself. Some people couldn't help themselves, always grinning like idiots. Or maybe he knows something I don't. His smiles and smug glances were really starting to get on my nerves.

As soon as we were in the air, I unbuckled my seatbelt and leaned forward. "Tell me the truth, Ronan. Who is that guy? What's he doing here with us?"

Ronan sighed and leaned to the side to let his chin rest on his fist. "This is my mother's doing. She's being over-protective. I told you she was this way, always sticking her nose in my business where it doesn't belong."

"She sent him to keep an eye on you?"

"Yes and no." He shifted his weight and leaned forward so we could whisper. "I'm sure he'll report every-thing I do back to her, but they aren't exactly friends. She sent him as a gesture of goodwill. He's supposed to assist in investigating what happened at the factory the other night."

I glanced at Vaughn, who'd opened a magazine. At least he wasn't grinning at me anymore. "Why him? He's not the most qualified investigator."

"He's a vampire, Callie."

The news made the hair on the back of my neck stand on end. "I wish you'd told me that before I was trapped in a metal tube thirty-five thousand feet in the air with him!"

"Calm down," Ronan whispered. "He's not going to do anything. Vaughn works for the vampire aristocracy. He's a liaison between his people and mine."

"*Your* people?"

He blinked and sat up. "Come on, you're pulling my leg. You *must* know."

I shook my head. "I have no idea what you mean. Models? Why would there need to be a liaison between vampires and underwear models? Do you guys have some sort of union?"

"God, you're serious." He rubbed his temples. "Fae, Callie."

I don't know why I was surprised. After hearing vampires were a thing, nothing should've shocked me, but you'd think he would've mentioned that before I signed on. Why would he expect me to know he was fae? Of course, Ronan had been scatterbrained all morning. Maybe he thought he'd told me and forgot.

I meant to say all of that out loud, but what came out of my mouth was, "Like Tinkerbell?"

Ronan slapped his palm to his face. "Why is that what everyone thinks of when they hear 'fae?' Do I look like I'm five inches tall in a green tutu to you? Have you ever seen me sprinkle magic gold dust?"

"How should I know? I just met you a few days ago, and it's not like you've spent any time explaining any of this to me. The only training I've had for this job has been pretty rushed. I've got to say, that's something you could work on."

"It's all in the book." He pointed to the book I'd placed on the empty seat next to me and sighed. "The book I didn't give you until this morning. Okay, fine. Fair enough. Look, we've got another hour and a half on this flight. Why don't we use it to clear all that up? If you have any questions, any at all, I'm happy to answer them."

"Wait a minute." My brain combed through our conversation the day before. "If you're fae, and your mother has the kind of clout to call up a high-ranking vampire and tell him to follow you around, you must be someone important."

Ronan sighed again, except this time, his body deflated

as the air left it. "My mother is the current head of the winter court."

"Which would make you what, a prince?"

He cringed. "Please don't call me that. I don't want anything to do with court politics. That's why I'm here and not with her. She's supposed to leave me out of it, but she doesn't seem to have gotten the memo."

I stared at Ronan. Not only was he not human, but he was fae royalty? I hadn't signed on for that. I was there to be a bodyguard to a model and an Instagram celebrity, not someone who might be a political target. Well, at least the vampire attack made sense now. There was a reason someone might go after him; it hadn't been random. I didn't know if that should've been as comforting as it was.

"I think I could use a drink." I got out of my seat and went to the back of the plane, where I'd spied a fully stocked minibar. Since I was on the job, I skipped the booze and grabbed a Coke from the fridge. It wasn't what I wanted, but it would have to do. As much as I desired a stiff drink to wash the taste of Ronan's news out of my brain, I wasn't going to give him or Vaughn any reason to question my ability to do my job.

"Enjoying the flight, Ms. Hart?" Vaughn asked from behind me. He'd stood up to stretch as I walked past him and had apparently followed me.

I turned around, soda in hand. "Are you?"

He shrugged and opened the little fridge I'd just stepped away from. "I have to say, I didn't wake up with the intention of going to New York this morning, but things change. In my position, you have to learn to be flexible."

Ronan had said you could tell a lot about a person from

their shoes, but that wasn't the only way to judge someone. I'd learned a long time ago that you could guess a lot about someone's personality based on the drinks they ordered. Boring people drank tea. Classy boring people drank hot tea. Normal people gravitated toward Coke or Pepsi, but anyone with taste picked the former over the latter whenever possible. Psychopaths and sociopaths drank weird things like grape and orange soda. The truly dangerous and unpredictable assholes? They'd cornered the Dr. Pepper market.

Vaughn grabbed the one and only Dr. Pepper in the fridge and gulped it down like a maniac.

I put my can of Coke down on the bar. "I know what you are."

"A vampire?"

"A bloodsucker of a different sort." I lowered my voice to make sure Ronan didn't hear. "Someone who likes conflict. You get off on pitting two people against each other and letting them fight it out. Then, when both sides are too decimated to resist, you swoop in and pretend to offer salvation. Every problem you solve is one of your own making. You're a snake in the grass, Vaughn. I've got my eye on you."

He laughed so hard he doubled over. When he recovered, he stood up and wiped a tear from the corner of his eye. "Well done, Ms. Hart! That was the most intimidating speech I've heard all day. I can see why he hired you. You do have a certain…arrogance. You two are alike in that regard." Vaughn swooped in, moving so fast I didn't have time to react. One minute he was an arm's length away from me, the next, he was right in front of me, so close I almost choked on his cologne. "You might think you have me figured out, but I promise you, I'm still full of surprises." He grinned his smug grin and took a step back, raising his can of Dr. Pepper in a toast. "I look forward to working closely with you in the future."

As I watched him walk back to his seat, I was more sure than ever that he and his company'd had something to do with what'd happened to me the night before, and probably the attack at the warehouse too. Before this was all said and done, I was going to make sure he regretted his involvement. All I needed was proof.

CHAPTER ELEVEN

I'd never been to New York City before, nor had I attended a professional photoshoot. It seemed the day was going to be full of firsts.

As soon as we'd landed at JFK, the three of us had been whisked away in another car with another driver. I wouldn't have to remember the names of his drivers. It was all stored in the new phone, logged in his receipts, his schedule, and his GPS.

The city was exactly like I'd expected it to be full of tall buildings, too many people, and choking smells. At the street level, everything smelled like car exhaust and distant food, although I could not tell if it was good food or rotten. Maybe it was both. Luckily, we didn't spend much time outside.

Vaughn had left us to do some business of his own once we reached the studio. We would call him when we were ready to head back to the plane.

I don't know what I expected a photography studio to look like, but it turned out to be a four-story brick building in Brooklyn with a stone façade. There were no signs out front announcing it was a studio of any kind. The building didn't even have a number on it. As far as I could tell, it was exactly like the other residential buildings around it. Once we got inside, though, it was very different. There wasn't any furniture, except for some folding chairs and a long folding table with a white tablecloth over it. It was empty except for a coffee and water dispenser.

A dark-haired woman in a bright red dress met us at the door. She had long hair, long enough that it must've taken hours to brush it. The way she swished it around when she walked said she was proud of it, as if growing hair was an accomplishment. Her name was Anna, and she turned out to be one of the production assistants, which I guessed was another name for 'glorified escort.' She brought us to a small dressing area so Ronan could change. Rather than dress for the photoshoot, however, he came out in a loose t-shirt and shorts, and they took us to a small gym area with a rack of free weights.

It seemed like a weird time for a workout, but I wasn't the pro. It wasn't my job to tell anyone what to do unless there was a dangerous situation, so I found a spot by the door and waited while Ronan went through a routine of pushups, lateral lifts, and curls.

After a few minutes, I noticed Anna inching closer to where I stood, arms crossed. She leaned to the side without taking her eyes off Ronan. "First photoshoot with Ronan?"

I looked her up and down and shrugged.

"Well, you're in for a treat. He is a darling to work with and the camera loves him, but it's not difficult when you look like that, am I right?" She giggled and elbowed me.

Seriously? Give me a break, lady. "I guess so. I'm just here to do my job, ma'am."

"Ma'am? My, aren't we professional? Let me guess: his new personal assistant?"

I turned so she could see the weapon holstered at my side. "Bodyguard."

"Oh." She inched away, reassessing me. "I didn't realize there were women bodyguards. It must be difficult. I don't think I'd be able to concentrate. I mean, look at him." She pulled out her phone and snapped a photo of him as he bent over to put down the weights. "Hashtag snacc!"

She typed it with two Cs. I thought I was going to gag.

Her thumbs hit the screen at a million miles an hour. "Oh, what's your Insta? I'll tag you to the photo."

"I don't do social media."

Anna stared at me as if I was some kind of alien, then slowly lifted her phone, took a photo of me, and went back to posting for her followers. "You're a rare breed in this day and age. Girl, I don't know how you do it. I would die if I couldn't log in for a day."

"Might want to talk to your doctor about that." I snatched the phone out of her hands.

"Hey! That's mine!"

She stood next to me complaining nervously but didn't make a move to try to get her phone back as I deleted the photo she'd taken of me. I hesitated for a minute, thumb hovering over the photo of Ronan she'd snapped. It was one thing for me to remove photos of myself, but maybe he didn't care. *Screw it. She could've asked.* I hit delete.

Once the photo was gone, I tossed the phone back to

her and went to open the door. "I'm afraid I'm going to have to ask you to wait outside."

She made an offended sound. "Hashtag rude!"

"Have a nice day, ma'am. We'll be with you shortly," I told her as I shut the door behind her.

"You should've let that slide," Ronan said. He'd apparently finished his workout and stood in the middle of the room, hands on his hips, one of his earbuds in his hand. "You won't be able to stop them all. Random fangirl photos kind of come with the territory."

"I've seen people look at a juicy steak the way she was looking at you. It was freaking me out. She was like a goddamn cannibal. I swear, it was getting creepy."

"Was it a good picture of my ass, at least?"

"I don't see what that has to do with—"

"If it was a good picture, you should've let her post it. I haven't had a good ass shot in a while. Everyone gets the upper body."

I stared at him. "She was talking in hashtags. Who does that? And what the hell is a 'snacc' with two Cs?"

Ronan laughed and popped out the other earbud, tucking both away and shaking his head. "First thing you're going to have to learn is to pick your battles, Callie. Going after everyone who snaps an unauthorized selfie with my ass in the background is going to wear you out. Come on. Hard part's done. Now all I have to do is get cleaned up and smile for the camera."

I sighed and followed him back into the dressing room. He disappeared behind a big privacy wall to clean up while I closed the door to the gym area and made sure it was securely locked. "Why the workout? Seems counter-intuitive to get dirty, only to get cleaned up again."

He turned on a sink. "It increases blood flow and helps the muscles bulk up. All about getting that stupid six-pack for the camera."

"Stupid, huh? Doesn't sound like you care much for it."

"Oh, I don't mind the work. Or the attention. Sometimes it gets old, being reduced to how you look, though. It's a cutthroat business, the male model world, especially if you're not a physically large person. I work out all the time, but bulking up and getting ripped is hard. I've got genetics working against me. Fae naturally tend toward being thinner. Some guys don't have to work at it." He came out from behind the privacy wall, having cleaned up and changed into a pair of simple black sweats and a white t-shirt.

"Listen, if I overstepped—"

"It's fine. You're new." He shrugged and slowly went to the door leading back to the studio. "Just remember, I can run my own personal life. If I wanted someone to get on my case about who I spend my time with, I'd call my mother."

The photoshoot took forever. They stuck Ronan on a weird green sheet that ran over the wall and floor and blasted him with bright lights from all directions. I don't know how he wasn't squinting the whole time.

As it turned out, he was more than just an underwear model. They dressed him in all kinds of clothes from khaki shorts to swim trunks to jeans, t-shirts, and sunglasses. It felt like someone was running in every few minutes to adjust some piece of clothing, fix the makeup on his cheeks, or brush his hair. Sometimes all three of them went on at once. Having so many people buzzing all around me, touching me all at once, would've pissed me off, but he just stood there, a living mannequin for people to dress, undress, and pose.

The guy behind the camera shouted directions as if his life depended on how fast people obeyed his orders. "Look off to the right. Lift your chin. I need more flex. Give me more apathy in the eyes. Now look like you want to fuck the camera. Now less. Rotate forty degrees. Ninety. More light. Less." The orders and camera flashes came so rapidly, I didn't know how anyone could possibly follow what was going on. To me it seemed like chaos, but everyone involved knew their parts by heart.

The entire time, Anna stood on the other side of the set, sending irritated glares my way. She might've been pissed at me, but she didn't try to sneak another photo during the shoot.

It was well into the afternoon by the time the photographer announced they were done, but even then, the work wasn't finished. Ronan went off to the side to sit with Anna and her boss, going over the photos. My phone buzzed with a notification he'd gotten an email, which turned out to be a bundle of the photos.

"For my agent," Ronan shouted to me from across the studio. "Do me a favor, Callie. Go through some of those and post a few?"

"Post a few?" I frowned. I didn't know the first thing about posting pictures on social media. I hadn't thought that would be part of the job description. Didn't he have people for that?

I was still scrolling through the photos when I felt a

tingle on the back of my neck. I looked up and spied movement in the dressing area, something glowing. No one else seemed to have spotted it. They were all bent over the camera, busy going through the rest of the photos. I put away my phone and went to check it out.

With my hand on my weapon, I carefully crept down the short hallway and stood by the cracked door, listening for movement. There was a dull buzzing sound inside, like a fluorescent lightbulb but louder. What in the world could that be? Slowly, I pushed the door open.

A large black circle stood in the center of the room like a doorway, ringed in electric blue.

What the hell? That hadn't been there before. I took a step forward to investigate, and the glowing ring rushed toward me and swallowed me whole.

The next thing I knew, I was standing under a hot sun carrying seventy pounds of gear with sand in places sand should never go. Pale brown outcroppings of rock piled up on my right and left, the path ahead a narrow choke point. We were supposed to be on alert for snipers above us, but the area had been calm for weeks, so we'd let our guard down.

Private James Xavier—affectionately known in the unit as Jax—walked beside me. We'd had the bad luck of pulling midday patrol duty. I much preferred night patrols because at least it was cool then, but good old Jax. Nothing could get him down. He was telling me a joke I'd heard a hundred times since boot camp.

"So a grunt and a sailor are in this nightclub on leave, right?" Jax said, squinting up at the sun. "They're both pissing at the urinals. Sailor finishes up and goes to wash his hands. Grunt zips up and heads straight for the door. Sailor says really loud from the sink, 'In Basic, they taught us to wash our hands after we piss.' And the grunt says—"

"In Basic, they taught him not to piss on his hands," I finished. "Heard that one. What else have you got?"

"You're such a bitch, Hart." Jax gave me a little shove.

"Takes one to know one." I gave him a harder shove back.

He laughed like a fool. "Man, you know what I miss?"

"Air conditioning? Apple pie? Sleeping in?" Everyone missed everything about civvy life. That was just how it was. Didn't matter how much you missed it, though, you learned fast enough not to bitch about it within earshot of your sergeant. Out there on patrol, that was where we did our best complaining. Might as well.

"Your mom." Jax giggled like a teenage girl.

I snorted. "Yeah, never heard that one before, either."

The radio clipped to my uniform kicked on. "Hotel, Juliet, what's your position?"

Hotel and Juliet were the designations for H and J respectively, the first letters of the names the squad called us.

"This is Juliet," Jax reported. "We are just south of the Devil's asshole, two o'clock to Bumfuck, Nowhere."

"Very funny," answered Trisco. "Movement near our position. Going to check it out. Rendezvous on me."

"Roger that. There in five."

"It's probably just another dog," I said. We'd been seeing a lot of them around the base lately. More than usual.

As Jax was getting ready to agree with me, the popcorn sound of machine gunfire erupted on the other side of the rock outcropping, and a report of shots fired came across the wideband radio.

"Callie!"

I exhaled and I was back in the studio, standing in the middle of the changing room.

Ronan was in front of me, his expression one of concern. He waved a hand in front of my face. "You okay?"

"Yeah, I think so." I shook my head and looked around for the portal, but it was gone. What the hell was that?

Ronan frowned. "You sure?"

"You didn't happen to see anything weird in here? Like a glowing light?"

Ronan glanced around the room and shook his head. "Are you feeling okay?"

Maybe the portal had never really been there. It could've been some sort of flashback triggered by the recent stress, but I wasn't sure. I'd never heard of anyone describing flashbacks as being like walking through a portal, and I hadn't ever had one before. Nightmares, sure, but never a flashback. Maybe that was all it was. Still, it felt like I had been dismissing too many weird happenings since I'd met Ronan, especially in light of the revelation that he was a fae prince. We still needed to talk about that.

He gripped my shoulder and squeezed. "It's late. You probably haven't eaten all day, have you? It's one thing for me to do that. I'm used to it, but you... Why don't we go grab something to eat? I know a great pizza place across town. Vaughn can catch up with us there."

I nodded. Pizza did sound good. "Sure."

The pizza place Ronan took me to was a small hole-in-the-wall with an authentic brick oven and a chef in the back who looked like he used to break knees with a baseball bat for a living. Black and white photos and framed newspaper clippings lined the walls of the narrow eatery, which only had six booths with red leather seats. After a long argument about me acting like the bodyguard I was and watching for threats, which he won, we opted for a place at the counter on a pair of stools covered with the same material. At least our backs weren't to the door since the counter was off to the side of the walk-up bar.

Despite the place's small size and unusual location, it was pretty busy. There were people at every booth when we came in, but they started to clear out shortly after our arrival. It was late, after all.

Ronan ordered a personal pizza with mushrooms, ham, chicken, and extra cheese. I got my favorite: crust and cheese, no sauce.

Ronan frowned at me as I handed the menu back to the guy at the counter. "That's not a pizza. You have to have tomato sauce on it to make it a pizza."

"It's round," I argued. "It has dough and cheese. Where is it written that a pizza must have tomato sauce?"

He turned to the kid behind the counter. "Tell her it has to have tomato sauce."

The kid shrugged. "Customer's always right."

"You're a monster," Ronan accused dryly. "You've created an abomination. I'm not sure I can sit here and watch you eat that, Callie. It's a sin against pizza."

I shrugged. "That's how I like it. Cheaper to order it that way, too. Sometimes pizza places will give you a discount if you don't want the sauce, although I'm sure that's not something you've ever had to worry about. You've always been loaded, being a prince and all."

"I know it must seem like my life is all sunshine and roses, but far from it."

I grunted. "If your only problem is an overbearing mother and potential assassination by vampires, I'd say you're pretty well off. You've never had to worry about paying rent. If your work dried up, you wouldn't be totally screwed. I don't mean to sound bitter, but yeah, your life sounds pretty good to me."

"Grass is always greener on the other side." He sighed and sipped the water he'd ordered. "Okay, then. Tell me what you'd do in my position. If money was no object, what would you be doing right now?"

I considered it for a moment, scanning the walls like I was searching for ideas. "Probably lounging on some beach in the Caribbean, sipping a ridiculous fruit-flavored drink I'd be embarrassed to drink anywhere else."

"A beach? That's cliché. Come on, you can do better. If I handed you a million-dollar check right now, you're telling me you'd blow it on mai tais, cabana boys, and beach vacations?"

He was right. The beach was probably what everyone said. The truth was, I'd seen enough sand for a lifetime. I shrugged. "Realistically, I think I'd buy a house. A car. Invest the rest. I'm pretty boring."

"What if you already had all that? Dream bigger. Go on. Anything you've ever wanted."

I studied his eager face for a minute and looked away. "You'll laugh."

"I won't. I promise. Come on, Callie. You spent the day watching random strangers strip me down, dress me up, and pose me like a doll. I'm not going to laugh at you for being honest."

I fiddled with the straw in my glass. "I've always wanted to go into space."

"Space?" He made a face. "Why?"

"Because it seems like it would be peaceful up there. Quiet. Serene. A good place to get perspective, you know?"

The kid behind the counter slid our pizzas onto the bar in front of us.

Ronan nodded to my pizza. "You need some perspective if you think that counts as a pizza."

"If we're going to critique each other's food choices, maybe you should think about cutting back on the calories if you want to maintain that figure of yours."

Ronan laughed and picked up the parmesan shaker. "Trust me, I'll be fine. My personal trainer might kill me if he knew I was eating this, but what he doesn't know won't hurt him. His routine is insane. I'm sure I'll burn it all off before the next shoot."

He picked up the pizza to take a bite.

I happened to look up before I grabbed mine and glanced into the big-screen TV. It was off, but I caught a glimpse of light reflecting off something metallic several stories up.

I reacted by instinct, tackling Ronan to the ground as the glass behind us shattered. A bullet whizzed past us, burying itself in the wall. I held him down for a minute, until I was relatively sure there weren't going to be any more shots coming, then sat up, drew my weapon, and tried to spot whoever had fired the shot.

A dark figure darted in front of a window in the building across the street, two stories up.

"Call the police!" I shouted to the kitchen staff. "Ronan, get behind the counter and don't move until I get back! I might have a line on the shooter." I really wished Vaughn had gotten here by now. I'd have to hire more guards if this was the way things were going to go. Without waiting for his argument, I shot to my feet and rushed out the door to dart across the street.

The building across from the pizzeria was an old apartment building undergoing renovations. The front door was blocked, so I raced around the side. At least I knew he wouldn't be exiting through there, though I didn't wait to check the back. Chances were good the shooter was already gone, but maybe I could catch him if I hurried.

I burst through the side door and took the dusty stairs two at a time. The movement in the window had been on the third floor, but once I reached it, I had to stop for a moment to get my bearings. He would've been in one of the rooms facing the pizzeria, and that whole wing of the building had been blocked off by heavy tarps. I pointed my gun at the ground and slid through them sideways, bringing my weapon up in case he was there waiting for me.

The hallway was clear, but that didn't mean the whole floor was. I'd have to go room to room to make sure he wasn't hiding up there, and the longer I was away from Ronan, the higher the chance that something else would happen.

I'll just clear the rooms in this hall, I thought and checked the closest one. It was dark and the lights weren't working, so I had to use a flashlight to check the darkened corners. One by one, I checked and cleared every room in the hall, finding no sign of the shooter until I reached the halfway point. There, I found a room with a spent shell casing. He must've been in a real hurry if he hadn't stopped to collect that. I was able to take a picture of the shell casing since the phone had a flash. Then something else caught my eye: a scrap of olive-green canvas caught on a nail near the door. It was the only other clue in the room. I studied it, but no matter how much I looked at it, it didn't tell me what it belonged to. I took a snap of that too.

A spent shell casing and a scrap of green canvas, I thought. It wasn't much to go on, but it was better than nothing.

CHAPTER TWELVE

I sat in the back of the jet near the minibar, looking at the pictures of the scrap of fabric and the shell casing. After the shooting, the police came and took statements from Ronan, me, and everyone else in the pizzeria, meaning it was after midnight when the plane finally took off. My stomach hadn't let me forget that I didn't get to take a bite before I saved Ronan's ass a second time. All I'd had to eat all day was a bag of chips I scarfed down on the plane.

The cabin lights were dim, but Ronan and Vaughn weren't asleep. I could hear their voices at the other end of the cabin, even if I couldn't make out what they were saying. As much as I wanted to hate Vaughn, he seemed as upset as the rest of us that someone had shot at Ronan. Since he showed up at the pizzeria, he'd been on the phone every few minutes, shouting at someone to get him surveillance footage. The police had confiscated it, of course, so we wouldn't be seeing the footage until after they finished their investigation. They had found the fabric and the shell casing I had referenced in my report, too.

The shell casing belonged to a .308 Winchester round. That seemed useful to know unless you were aware that the .308 was one of the most common rounds in the United States, used both for military applications and deer hunting. Considering the distance and trajectory of the shot, however, I didn't think our shooter was taking potshots at Ronan with a hunting rifle. The bullet had missed him only because I saw the flash of light in the television screen. If I hadn't looked up right when I did, he'd be dead.

The fabric seemed more helpful. It was just a scrap of green canvas, exactly as I thought, but there weren't many things in the world made from that type of canvas. The texture and weave of the fabric reminded me of my old duffel bag, and maybe it was. That'd be the perfect way to conceal a sniper rifle. If the shooter was fast and well-trained, he could've had that rifle apart and packed in the bag in seconds. He'd probably gone out a side or back entrance before I was in the building.

This was no chump off the street. He was a pro. This wasn't the only shot that had been fired in my direction lately. There had been the one at the club. Where had that bullet gone? Into the cement wall? Maybe it was still there, or maybe the shell casing was. After two days it'd be hard to find—if I could find it at all—but maybe the police would get a match if they compared the two.

Vaughn stood and, phone to his ear, and paced toward the back of the plane. "I want the entire unit standing by when we land. Clear the entire terminal and sweep any vehicles with a direct line of sight on our landing strip." He paused beside the minibar. "Well then, send a plain-clothes squad in. You're not going to win an argument with the TSA, and I'm not calling the President twice in one week. I have better things to do than sit on hold for an hour." His phone beeped as he hung up. "Idiots, all of them."

I put my phone on dark. "You know I would coordinate security on the ground if I thought it was necessary. No one is going to shoot at him at the airport. Security there is pretty tight."

"On that, we agree, Miss Hart, but I must be seen to be doing something." He shook his head and popped the top on another Dr. Pepper. "This is a public relations night-mare for me—first the vampire attack in Columbus, and now this. Lucky you were there with him when it happened. Meanwhile, I was stuck in Manhattan traffic."

"Working on your investigation into what happened at Kloud9?"

"I wish all my cases were that simple. No, there were people to appease in New York too, I'm afraid." He sipped from the can as if it were a glass of wine. "There hasn't been much news about the Kloud9 event, nor do I expect there to be. It was an isolated attack, and the fuss about it will calm down soon enough."

I raised an eyebrow. "An isolated event? Someone shot at him today too, Vaughn."

"There's no proof those two events are related—as I've been telling everyone else." He waved his phone at me. "It's unlikely a vampire would've used a gun, especially if he wanted to get a message across, which is the only real reason to attack someone like Ronan. He's not a tactical target."

"But he's royalty. That automatically makes him a tactical target."

Vaughn smirked. "Not as such. He's got no stake in the court other than his blood. He's barely involved in politics, although killing him would upset the queen. Then again, that's not hard to do. She can be...unstable."

I pushed up from my seat and went to the little bar. In addition to all the drinks, the bar was stocked with packaged snacks like cookies and chips. It wasn't enough to call it a meal—that would have to wait until after we'd landed —but I was starving. I grabbed a package of chocolate chip cookies and tore it open. "Speaking of unstable, I ran into some of your people the other day."

"My people?"

"A bunch of vampires tried to jump me outside a dance club in Columbus. Kinda funny, isn't it? First, they're at the place where I work, then they show up while I'm out with a friend, having a good time?"

Vaughn stared at me, unimpressed by my insinuation. "Let me be clear. I'm not in control of every vampire in the world, nor am I responsible for their actions. You drew attention to yourself when you killed one of us, Ms. Hart. Perhaps the vampire who attacked you was a friend of the one you killed." He tipped his can as if to take another drink.

I snatched the Dr. Pepper out of his hand and placed it on the bar. "I know you know more about what's going on than you've said, Vaughn. I saw the Meyer Securities van parked outside the club. That can't be a coincidence. It also can't be a coincidence that someone fired a shot outside the club last night. I'd be very interested to see if the ballistics match what I found at the pizzeria scene."

"I have no idea what you're talking about." He took his drink back and tried to make his escape.

I swooped around the bar, blocking his exit. "You expect me to believe you're so bad at your job that you didn't know about the attack outside the nightclub? I know it didn't make the news. Someone cleaned it up before it did. Your company's van was at the scene, Vaughn. Don't treat me like I'm stupid."

He snorted and pushed past me. "I've got nothing to say to you."

"I don't care that a couple of your idiots roughed me up, Vaughn," I called after him, loud enough that Ronan turned to look at us.

Vaughn froze in place, sighed, and turned around. "What do you want?"

I stepped closer so I didn't have to shout. "I want to know what sort of bullet you recovered from the nightclub parking garage."

"I am not at liberty to discuss internal matters with you." He buttoned his jacket and lifted his chin.

"If someone's taking shots at me, they might be the same person shooting at Ronan. Based on what I recovered from the scene, we could be dealing with someone dangerous. Someone who knows their way around weapons as well as I do, who looks at a city block and sees a battlefield. He looks at you and at me, and all he sees are targets in his way. Now, are you going to help me figure out who this guy is, or are you going to stand there with your plausible deniability, looking like an incompetent asshole?"

He narrowed his eyes and sipped his Dr. Pepper, buying himself a minute to think it over. After a long stare-down, he bought his phone back out, hit a button, and put it to his ear. "This is Vaughn. Did you run the ballistics for the parking garage incident yet? I see. Yes. Understood. Thank you." He hung up and tucked the phone back into his breast pocket. "The bullet that was recovered appears to have been a .308 round. Not very useful information, but there you have it."

"That's more useful than you realize." I slid back into my seat, crossing my arms. "It's the same type as the shell casing I found in the building across from the pizzeria. It could mean it was the same shooter."

"Or it could mean nothing." Vaughn eyed Ronan carefully. Ronan was watching our conversation with interest. "It's one of the most common bullets in the world, used by law enforcement, big game hunters—"

"And would-be fae prince assassins, it would seem," Ronan added, leaning on his fist.

"There's more." I hopped back up, passed Vaughn, and went to sit across from Ronan, holding out the scrap of canvas I'd found. "I think this is part of a duffel bag. It's a military issue duffel bag. Could be what the shooter is carrying his weapon around in."

Ronan took the scrap of fabric and turned it over. "What does that mean? He's in the military?"

"Maybe." I shook my head. "Hard to say. You can buy those things at military surplus stores, so it could belong to someone playing at being a soldier, or just someone with good taste in duffel bags."

Vaughn grunted.

I ignored him. "We can draw some conclusions about the shooter with this information, though. It's enough to make me worry that you're right about being in serious danger. I'd like to call in some extra security once we get back. Maybe I should stay there. Supervise and get to know the rest of the team."

I hadn't met the part-timers on Ronan's security team yet, but I had glanced at their dossiers on the plane earlier. They weren't former military, but they had limited security experience. Both were guys, and young enough this was probably just a paycheck for them on the weekends and overnights while they got through college. While their files suggested they took the job seriously enough to keep Ronan alive, I didn't think either of them would jump in front of a bullet for him.

That's what I did earlier, I realized for the first time. I hadn't even thought about it. I could've died.

Ronan sighed. "I think it'll be good for you to get to know the rest of the team, but maybe not tonight. I'm exhausted. I'm not going anywhere, and I'll keep the shutters closed. With all the security in place at the house, it should be enough to keep anyone from getting in. Besides, if anything happens, they'll hit the panic button, and you'll be alerted on your phone." He patted my shoulder. "You should get some sleep. I need you in top condition tomorrow."

"Why? What's happening tomorrow? Another photoshoot?"

"No." He relaxed limply into the seat. "Good thing too. I need a day to recover. But considering everything that's going on, I'd rather have you at one hundred percent tomorrow than running on empty tonight."

"I'll speak to your mother," Vaughn offered.

"I couldn't care less what you do, Vaughn. Just get this settled before it gets farther out of control. I don't like being this close to court politics. The sooner we can put all this behind us, the better for us all."

The seatbelt light came on. Vaughn took his seat, and we all strapped in for the landing. I looked out the window, taking in the Columbus skyline in the dark and wondered how the hell I'd gotten myself into this mess.

CHAPTER THIRTEEN

After we touched down, Vaughn met with his people, collected them, got into one of his company vans, and sped away without saying much to us. Ronan and I piled into the back of the waiting car. He was so tired, he fell asleep on the short drive across town. I wasn't far behind him. Of course, I couldn't pass out as soon as we got back. I needed to get in my car and drive back to the loft.

I checked the time on my phone. If I drove five over the speed limit, I could be home in time to get two whole hours of sleep before I had to be back up and ready for work. So much for one hundred percent functionality. Oh, well. I'd survived longer on less sleep while I was overseas.

We came to the gate, and the car stopped. It took me a minute to realize the driver was waiting for one of us to open it with the app on our phones. Ronan had fallen asleep, so it was up to me. I fumbled to get my phone out and press the gate open button.

I groaned as we pulled up to the door and I got a good

look at the house. None of the lights were on, and there weren't any cars in the guest parking area except for mine. The night guard hadn't shown up for his shift. One day on the job, and my employees were already testing my patience.

Ronan woke up with a sharp intake of breath as soon as the car stopped. "Are we back?"

"Stay here for a minute." I opened the door.

"Why? What's wrong?"

I gestured to the parking area. "The night guard's car isn't here. I'll check out the house and give you the all-clear to enter if it's safe." I was so going to look into hiring more guards in the morning. I had to keep leaving him alone to do my job, and that wasn't acceptable. I also realized being a soldier and a security guard were not the same as being a bodyguard, so I was going to look into getting some training, or at least find time to read Walter's book.

With my flashlight out, I went to the front door and used my phone to unlock it. I was starting to love how much I could do with that phone, but that also meant anyone with the right password could do the same.

The front room was empty. I switched on the light and went to the next part of the house, moving through the rooms one by one to check for intruders. It was unlikely anyone was in there. If the front door or the gate had been opened while we were away, both Ronan and I would've gotten a notification on our phones. But there were vampires in the world now, and other things. Who knew if all the monsters out there needed a door to get in?

I walked into the kitchen and reached for the light. A flash of white sailed through the air, straight for my face.

On instinct, I held my hand out. Just before hitting me, the buzzing white dispersed around me, spreading and crackling into a dome of ice. I pulled my gun and fired, shattering the ice in front of me, but not before another shot careened out of the darkness toward me. I caught it like a ball and watched in wonder as the magic spun in my palm, forming a thin coat of frost over my skin. It lasted only a moment before the spell fell apart, melting like ice.

I readied for another attack.

"What the hell's going on in here?" Ronan hit the light switch to my right.

The intruder was a tall woman with pale, delicate features. She wore a sparkling blue dress in a style that wasn't common outside renaissance faires. Bright red hair fell in tight coils over her shoulders. She stood with one arm outstretched, her face twisted with malice.

Ronan blinked. "Mom? What are you doing here?"

Mom? I looked from the intruder to Ronan. She didn't look old enough to be his mother, but then again, they were fae. Maybe they didn't age like normal people. If I looked hard enough, I could see the similarities in their features.

Then it dawned on me what I'd done. I'd pulled my gun and aimed it at a faerie queen.

"Put that down." Ronan pushed my gun toward the floor.

I stumbled through trying to explain myself. "I thought —I mean, she was—"

"She's not going to hurt me any more than she already has." Ronan grunted and went to the stove to get the kettle. "If we're going to stand around, let's at least have some tea."

"Yes," said the faerie queen, "and you can introduce me to your…" She rolled her hand as if she were trying to think of the word. "Well, she doesn't look like one of your conquests."

"Callie, Mab. My mother. Mom, Callie Hart, my new head of security." Ronan mumbled through the introductions while he filled the kettle and put it on the stove.

"Security?" Mab lifted her chin and reevaluated me. "I see."

"Speaking of security, why isn't David on shift?" I asked, folding my arms.

Mab dismissed my question with a wave of her hand. "I gave him the night off. Now, Ronan, we need to talk about this Callie girl. She doesn't bear the mark of a court."

"I'm aware of that, Mother."

"And she threw my spell back at me."

"I saw."

"You know I'm standing right here, right? I can hear everything you're saying." I holstered my gun and flashlight.

Mab chose to ignore me in favor of going to Ronan. She spun him around and took his face in her hands. "Let me look at you. It's been so long since I've gotten to see you, my son. I've almost forgotten what you look like."

He batted her away. "We just talked two days ago!"

"A video chat is not the same thing as a face-to-face meeting!"

"I'm too busy to fly up to see you all the time. You know that." He tried to escape by going to the fridge and opening it.

Mab waited on the other side of the open door, arms

crossed. "Yes, busy flitting around the country and posing half-naked for humans to gawk at."

"We've discussed this, Mother. Modeling is my job, and I like my job." He closed the fridge, a jug of milk in hand. "I'm not quitting because you don't like it."

I cleared my throat. "Look, if you're safe, Ronan, maybe I should—"

"Have some tea first. It'll help you wake up for the drive home." He gave me a desperate look. Poor guy really did not want to be left alone with his mother, but I wasn't sure what help I'd be.

Still, he was my employer, and I had saved him from an assassin earlier in the day. The least I could do was be there for moral support. "Okay. Am I still on the clock?"

"Yes," Ronan replied.

"No," Mab snapped at the same time.

Ronan glared at her. "Last I checked, I pay my own employees, and you have no say in that, Mother."

"And the last I checked, you enjoy your comfortable lifestyle at my pleasure. One word from me and you'll actually need to work for a living, son." She gave him a vicious smile.

Ronan sighed, crossed his arms, and leaned against the counter. The two of them stared each other down until the tea kettle whistled. Ronan turned his back to her, busying himself making three cups of tea. "Why are you here?" He held a cup out to her.

"I heard about the assassination attempt in New York, of course." Mab took the tea and retreated a safe distance, standing halfway between Ronan and me. She blew on her cup, and it frosted over. "I tried to call, but you rejected all my attempts. Since Walter's gone, I couldn't call him, so I decided to come down and see you. It's been eight months since we spoke in person, Ronan. You look thin. Have you been eating?"

"I'm fine. Callie is taking good care of me." He crossed the kitchen, making sure to walk around the other side of the island rather than in front of Mab.

"Yes," said Mab. "I heard she intervened at the factory. That whole mess could've been avoided if security at Kloud9 had been in order. You let a vampire walk in and assault my son."

I took the steaming cup from him and tried to shrink into a corner while the fae queen stared me down. "I didn't know I should be watching out for vampires, and no offense, Your Highness, but I've saved Ronan's life twice this week. I think I'm doing pretty well."

"It's 'Your Majesty,'" she corrected and sipped her tea. "Handling a crisis with dignity doesn't excuse being the cause of said crisis, my dear. Though you've done well for yourself, haven't you? Came out of it on top."

Ronan lowered his teacup and squinted at her. "What are you insinuating?"

"Stop it," I growled with more force than I intended.

Both of them stared at me.

I sighed. "Listen, it's almost three o'clock in the morning. I'm tired. I'm sore. I just learned that vampires are a thing and had magic thrown at me. I chased an assassin through a building, and I've barely eaten or drunk anything all day. No offense, but at this hour, I can't deal with drama." I turned to Ronan and placed the tea on the kitchen island next to him. "Thanks for the tea. I'll check the rest of the house before I go. It was nice meeting you, ma'am." I gave the queen my best approximation of a curtsy and removed myself from the kitchen.

"Callie, wait. Don't leave mad."

I stopped when Ronan chased me as far as the front room. "I'm not mad. Just...overwhelmed, and a little insulted."

He sighed and shook his head. "Don't let her get to you. She's just like that. Why do you think we don't talk?"

"Because you delight in torturing your poor mother?" Mab had followed him.

Ronan had enough and went to take his mother by the arm. "I'm glad you came, Mom, but it really is late. We can catch up over breakfast in a few hours. How's that?"

"As long as you're not cooking," Mab said as he opened the door. She turned to whisper to me, "His cooking is dreadful."

"Goodbye, Mom." Ronan half-shoved her out the door.

Mab clearly wasn't ready to go. She gripped the doorframe and held on to give me one last glance. She smiled and turned to her son. "Win this one for us, my dear."

"Good night." Ronan swung the door closed, forcing her to step back or get smacked in the face.

She took the first option.

Ronan locked the door and turned the security system back on. "I'm really sorry about her. She means well, but she's awful when she gets like this."

I frowned at the closed door. "What did she mean, 'Win this one for us?'"

He sank into the closest chair with a sigh but didn't

answer my question. "Callie, I'm tired. Let's do this another time."

"Oh, no. You're not getting off that easy." I turned on him. "You've been hiding something from me since the beginning. What did she mean? And why did you believe I already knew you were a fae prince?"

"I think you know the answers to those questions, Callie."

"You can't keep treating me like I know things, Ronan. I don't. You've got to stop hiding stuff from me if you want to do my job effectively."

He sighed again and pushed up from the chair, going to the door. I expected Mab to still be out there, waiting on the front porch when he pulled it open, but there was no sign of her. "Look, we can talk about this later, but right now, I think we both need to get some sleep. I'll see you around noon. Don't worry about coming in until then."

"But—"

"I'll call one of the part-timers," he offered and gestured to the door.

I clenched my fists. He wasn't going to listen to me, no matter what. "Fine," I growled and pulled out my phone. "But I'll call someone in. At least let me do my job."

"Whatever." He threw his hands up and walked away, leaving the door open. "I'm going to bed. Do whatever you want. I don't know why I thought you'd do anything else." He walked away, grumbling to himself.

That's a funny way to treat the woman who saved your life twice in one week, I thought and shut the door.

CHAPTER FOURTEEN

I stayed until David showed up. It must have been the other guard at the factory, since I didn't recognize him. As it turned out, Mab had indeed called and told him not to bother coming to work. After a brief introduction and instructions to keep Ronan in the house until I got back no matter how much he complained about it, I left.

The sun was on the verge of coming up as I drove across town, suppressing yawns with every mile. At least Ronan had told me I didn't have to come back in until noon, which meant I might get five glorious hours of sleep. If Sam went to class, that was. Dammit, it was Wednesday, wasn't it? Sam didn't have class on Wednesdays until the afternoon. That meant they'd be hanging out, expecting me to be personable. I was sure Sam would have a plethora of questions to ask me about my first full day on the job, but I was too tired to answer them.

Sam, being the insane insomniac they were, was already up when I arrived and waiting by the door with coffee.

"Bless you," I muttered, taking the mug. The coffee

wouldn't keep me up, but maybe long enough to drag myself through the shower.

Sam hung out near the door to the bathroom, sipping coffee while I took a hot shower. "So, tell me about it. Where'd you go? What'd you do?"

"Stuff and things," I answered with a grunt, resting my head against the shower wall.

Should I tell Sam someone took shots at Ronan? That'd just make them worry, but then again, Sam had a right to know, especially since the vampires didn't seem to be limiting their attacks to Ronan. I'd already had one run-in with them, and if Sam hadn't taken off when they did, they'd have been right there with me when the vamps attacked. It was only a matter of time before Sam figured out what was going on. If I'd been more alert, I might've spilled everything, but it took all my energy to get through the shower and put on my sweats.

Sam must've gotten the hint when all my answers were grunts or variations thereof. They left me alone and let me crawl into bed. I thought I was tired enough I'd fall right asleep and stay that way until the alarm went off, but I woke up after two hours and couldn't get back to sleep. With nothing to do, I went out to the living room and joined Sam, who was watching some idiots be really bad at a game show. While Sam ate cereal and yelled at the contestants for bidding too much on wrong answers, I dragged out the book Ronan had given me to read.

He said all the answers I wanted were in that thing. Too bad it was so dry, I almost fell asleep again while reading it. Walter might've been paranoid enough to do his job well and had decent taste in guns, but he wasn't a writer by any means.

Sam picked up the remote and turned the volume way down on a commercial break. "So, where'd you go? I want to hear all about it."

I finished skimming a paragraph on the importance of situational awareness in the restroom before I answered. "Photoshoot in New York."

"Oooh, sounds exciting."

I shrugged. "Not really. It was mostly me being a third wheel while everyone gawked at him. I was bored out of my mind." I shut the book. "Actually, no. Something did happen. Some asshole shot at us."

Sam's eyes doubled in size. They froze with a spoonful of cocoa balls halfway to their mouth, milk dripping back into the bowl. "Shut. Up!"

"And there was someone in the house when we got back. Turned out to be his crazy mother, of all people. Still, I saved his ass. You'd think he'd be a little nicer to me. Instead, he gives me this." I picked up the book and let it fall to the floor with a loud thud. "This is torture."

"You should try taking Spinesta's Theories of Modern Art." Sam snorted and crunched their cereal. "You'd think a course about art would be mostly visual, but no! He had us reading biographies and watching this God-awful biopic on this artist in San Francisco. It was two hours of some Boomer whining about how millennials are killing performance art."

I pulled my legs up to sit cross-legged in the chair. "It's not even the reading. It's that he's so blasé about everything. The guy gets shot at, and his biggest care in the world is how his hair looks when he gets off the plane. Here I am, trying to do my job, and he's taking selfies and tagging locations. I'll tell you what. If I was a would-be assassin, the first thing I would do is follow him on Instagram. That way, I'd know exactly where he was and what he was up to all the time. I swear he must've made twenty posts yesterday." I pulled out my phone and held it out to them. "And look, two already today. Does this guy even sleep?"

"Do you?" Sam got up to take their bowl to the sink, where they rinsed it out and dropped it in the dishwasher. "That's the pot calling the kettle black, Callie."

"I suppose." I frowned down at the screen and scrolled through everything he'd posted the day before. "I just can't shake the feeling that he's lying to me about something. Something important. No matter how much I push him on it, he won't tell me, and it's driving me crazy."

Sam grabbed the phone out of my hands as they passed by and hopped up to sit on the arm of our worn-out sofa. Their thumbs slid over the screen, scrolling over all the pictures I'd just looked at. "This is why you should be hitting that."

"He's my boss, Sam."

"So? Look at this." They turned the phone around, showing me an underwear ad campaign Ronan had featured in last year. "He's hotter than lava. He's rich. Bet you fifty bucks he's got an off-limits room in his house he calls a playroom."

"This isn't *Fifty Shades*, Sam. That's not how it works in real life." I grabbed the phone back. "Even if it was, that movie is awful."

"Fine. Let's compare him to a movie you like. You like *Rambo*, right?"

"Screw you. You know I hate that movie."

"Okay, then, Miss Film Critic. What movies *do* you like?"

I tried to think of the last movie I'd seen. "*Wonder Woman?*"

Sam wrinkled their nose. "Of course that's what you'd pick. Is there even a romantic subplot in that one?"

"Is that what we were talking about?"

Sam finally picked up the remote and shut off the TV, which neither of us was watching. "My point is, if you want a guy to spill a secret, that's the best way. Works every time. People are more likely to tell secrets after sex."

"I don't think that's 'people,' Sam. I think it's you."

"True." Sam put a finger to their chin. "No wonder you never tell me any secrets."

"Besides," I continued, bending over to pick up the book I'd dropped, "Ronan's not my type. He's..."

"Charming, sexy, and filthy-rich?"

"He reads Dickens and plays the violin. The guy is a nerd girl's dream." I flipped through the pages, absently looking for an interesting section to read. "Never mind that it would compromise my ability to do my job effectively if there were any sort of romantic attraction between us. And don't even get me started on how complicated my life would get if I were any more involved with him than I already am. His personal life seems to be a mess. Plus, the minute things stop being professional between Ronan and me, he'll lose respect for my abilities as a bodyguard."

"I hear you," Sam said, nodding. "But nowhere in there do I hear 'I don't want to bone my boss.'"

I looked up from the book and said firmly, "I can't guard a body I'm sleeping with, Sam. That's final."

Sam was about to make another rebuttal when my phone went off. I picked it up. Anything would be a welcome reprieve from the current conversation, even the unexpected email I'd just gotten. "Huh. That's weird. It's from Jax."

"Jax?"

"Guy from my unit."

Sam snorted and giggled. "Sorry. You said 'unit.'"

I ignored Sam's chuckling since they found humor in the oddest things and opened the email. It'd been months since I'd heard from him, and I had been starting to worry that he might not be okay. Poor guy'd had it much rougher than me. His wife had divorced him almost as soon as he came back, taking their daughter to Iowa, where she was from.

The last time we spoke, he'd just been evicted from his apartment and was having trouble finding steady work. While I'd gotten out of the military mostly unscathed, he'd been badly hurt. Jax had been the only one to survive the attack on our unit, myself excluded. Unlike Jax, though, I hadn't gotten hurt. He'd spent almost a month in the hospital before they discharged him. Looking at him, you could barely tell he'd been attacked, thanks to all the skin grafts, but in the right light, you could still see the scars on his neck and chin. He'd always been self-conscious about how he looked.

Jax had lost everything, and I worried about him a lot.

Sometimes it seemed the only thing keeping him sane was our weekly chats. Over time, those turned into monthly chats, then just the occasional email. I hadn't heard from Jax in almost four months now.

The email he sent sounded positive. Apparently, he was back in town after some time away and wanted to meet for drinks tomorrow night before he had to leave again. I sent him a quick reply, saying that sounded great, and suggested a venue.

"Setting up a date?" Sam made kissing sounds.

I snorted and put the phone down. "Dating Jax would be like dating my younger brother. I'm going to go see if I can get another hour of shut-eye before I have to go back to work. I think the reading has convinced me I need it."

I took the book with me to my bedroom and slid it under the bed. If there were any answers to my questions hidden in there, I hadn't found them. Ronan was just going to have to suck it up and explain things to me the old-fashioned way.

CHAPTER FIFTEEN

I went back to bed but couldn't sleep. For some reason, the only thing I could think about was the weird flashback I'd had at Ronan's photoshoot—if it *had* been a flashback. It hadn't felt like one; it had felt like a bad dream. I just couldn't figure out why I would start having them now after so long. PTSD was a common affliction among soldiers, and it wouldn't be unusual for me to have some of the symptoms, especially after everything I'd seen.

Except it shouldn't have taken years to manifest. Those things were supposed to happen when you got home. I'd watched Jax disintegrate when he started having flashbacks. He and I had even talked about it, and I'd helped him find a good therapist so he could get through his messy divorce. Flashbacks, PTSD, visions—those things didn't happen to me.

All this worrying is giving me a headache. I sat up in bed and rubbed my temples. It was ten thirty, only fifteen minutes before I was supposed to be up and getting ready for work. Might as well go caffeinate.

I left the bedroom, expecting to find Sam where I had left them, on the sofa watching television. Instead, the apartment was eerily empty. The skin on the back of my neck prickled. I put a hand to it and told myself it was the lack of sleep. "Sam? You here?"

Silence answered.

Something moved in the kitchen, and I sighed. "Sam, you ass. Why didn't you answer me when I…"

My voice trailed off when I came around the corner and found the kitchen empty of everything except another shimmering portal. What the hell is happening to me? What are these things? I let go of the wall to back away, but as before, the portal rushed toward me.

The next thing I knew, I was sitting in an uncomfortable chair in a hot room under a bright light. Two officers sat across the table from me, their hair perfect and eyes cold and calculating. Practically inhuman. The back of my head ached in that special way only concussions hurt, and the pressure around my skull told me there were bandages in place.

"Private Hart," said the officer on the right, adjusting his glasses. "Do you read a lot of books?"

"No, sir." I shifted in my chair. "The occasional paperback when things are slow, but everyone does that."

He looked up from the paper he was holding. "Your report sounds like one of my wife's romance novels."

The other officer read some of it aloud. "Private Xavier and I came around the rock formation while on patrol. I heard Private Jensen call out, then a burst of gunfire. By the time I arrived, he was already bleeding out. I attempted to apply first aid while Private Xavier kept watch, but was unsuccessful. Private Xavier called out a warning, and I turned in time to see something attack him. The perpetrator was bipedal and moved faster than I was able to perceive. It bit him in the throat and the side of the face before either of us could react. I believed Private Xavier, as well as the rest of my unit, to be DOA." He lowered the paper and folded his hands. "This thing attacked and bit everyone else in your unit, but all you got was a bump on the head. Makes it a little hard to believe, don't you think?"

"I don't know why it didn't attack me, sir. I thought..."

"Go on, Hart," encouraged the first man with the glasses. "We're here to get to the bottom of this."

I swallowed and nodded. "I am, or I was, the only female in my unit, sir. I thought maybe that was why. This thing wasn't human, even if it looked like it. It had to be an animal, right? No human could move that fast."

The two officers exchanged a look.

I leaned forward, placing one hand on the table. "What about Jax?"

"Private Xavier's condition is none of your concern." The second officer picked up his papers and tapped them against the table, straightening them before he stood. "Just one more question, Private Hart. Who else have you told? Who else knows what happened out there?"

"I've told you who knows," I said, leaning back. My heart thumped in my chest. Was that a mistake? Had I seen something I wasn't supposed to see?

"Good," said the officer, and he ripped the file folder in half. "Debrief her." The door slid open with a hiss, and he disappeared through it.

"Sir," I said, turning to the other officer, "Jax was like a brother to me. If he's gone, I deserve to know."

He sighed through his nose and pressed his lips together. "Jax's injures were severe, but it looks like he's going to pull through. No reason for you to worry, though. You're both going home."

I jumped out of my seat so fast the chair fell over. "Going home? As in, discharged? Sir—"

"It's an honorable discharge," he offered, raising his hands as if that'd calm me. "Not uncommon with severe head trauma. There are plenty of soldiers who would love to go home early. Don't look a gift horse in the mouth, Hart."

I woke up in my own bed, shivering despite my blankets. A bad dream? I touched my forehead. It didn't feel like a dream. It felt like...it felt like before, when I went through the portal at the photoshoot. What the hell was going on with me?

I exhaled and paused when I realized I could see my breath. That shouldn't have been possible. I knew we'd paid the heating bill.

There was nothing to do but get up and plod out to the living room. Maybe Sam had opened a window some-where and left it open. I checked the house, pausing when I wandered within sight of the kitchen. There was no sign of a shimmering portal anywhere or any indication that there had ever been one. Maybe it had been a dream.

It could be stress, I thought, pouring the cold coffee

from earlier into a mug. I popped the mug into the microwave to warm it up. Stress could cause all kinds of weird symptoms, from full-body rashes to hallucinations. Over the last few days, I'd experienced more stress than normal. Not only was there an assassin trying to kill my new boss, but I'd also been fired from my previous job and had to take a new one in an adjacent field, doing work I hadn't ever done before. While being a bodyguard was similar to working in corporate security in a lot of ways, there was a lot to take in. Plus, Ronan wasn't the most forthcoming guy.

Then there were the vampires. A few days ago, I hadn't known vampires and fae were real, yet there I was, working for fae royalty and rubbing elbows with asshole vampires like Vaughn. My world had been turned upside-down in the last few days.

Imagine how different my life will be next week? I pulled the coffee from the microwave just before the timer went off, dumped it in my travel mug, and left it to cool while I went to get dressed for work. I just hoped Ronan was less grumpy today than he had been the night before.

CHAPTER SIXTEEN

Even though he'd told me his schedule the night before, I checked the app Ronan had instructed me to use. He didn't have a photoshoot that day, which was a good thing. I didn't think I could handle getting on another plane and going to another city. When I'd said I wanted to travel, I hadn't meant as someone's bodyguard. That beach and those cabana boys were sounding better every minute.

Unlike the first two days, I didn't find Ronan in his music room. It had been shut up tight. Instead, he was lounging in the library in a pair of white loose-fitting pants and a matching robe...or a cardigan. I couldn't tell which it was supposed to be. He looked like he hadn't slept much either, despite kicking me out the night before.

"Reading more Dickens?" I asked.

He lowered the book and rubbed his eyes. "No, this is Dumas." Ronan tossed the book to me. "You might like it."

"*The Count of Monte Cristo*," I read from the cover. "I've heard this story."

"Hearing it and reading it are two different things. No one tells it like Dumas."

"No, thanks." I handed the book back to him. "I've got enough reading to do. Did you sleep at all?"

"Some." The way he said it made me think he really meant "not much." Ronan stretched. "I see you wore practical shoes today."

I looked down at the dress flats I'd slipped on. Standing around in heels, low though they were, had left my feet throbbing the day before, and I wasn't in the mood to repeat that mistake. The flats were functional and dressy enough that I didn't look unprofessional.

"That's good," he continued, striding out of the library. "Since I don't have any photoshoots today, I thought we'd go for a walk. The weather's still nice enough, and I'm already tired of being cooped up in here."

I cringed. Walking around town would make my job much more difficult. I couldn't account for every variable. No matter where we went, another shooter could be hiding just out of sight. "You'll be safer if you stay home."

Ronan paused at the bottom of the stairs. "Maybe, but where's the fun in always being safe? Safe is boring. I want to live my life." He started up the stairs.

I followed. "Now you sound like my roommate."

"Maybe you should listen to her."

"Them."

He paused again at the top of the stairs, frowning. "You have more than one roommate?"

"No, it's just, Sam prefers to be called 'they' instead of a binary pronoun. Actually, you two would get along great. Sam's an art student at OSU."

"I'd love to meet them once my schedule clears. Right now, I'm going to shower and get dressed for our walk. I don't think I need an escort."

I realized I'd been following him to his private suite and stopped in the middle of the hall, flushing. "Oh, uh, I guess I'll go watch the cameras. Let me know when you're ready to go."

While he showered and got ready, I checked the logs. David noted it was a quiet night and doodled an alien in the margins of the logbook. Must've been pretty slow if he'd had time to make a drawing with that much detail.

Since there wasn't much to do, I got started on the list of things I needed. It was longer than I'd expected it to be. I hesitated with my hand over the send button in my email after I finished it. If Ronan bought everything on that list, it'd total several thousand dollars easily. He wasn't struggling financially, but I had to take a minute to appreciate that I could just ask for something, and he'd make sure I got it. That wasn't the sort of treatment I would've gotten working overnight security for Kloud9. As far as jobs went, maybe this one wasn't so bad.

"Ready to go?"

I looked up from the computer. Ronan had already put on his coat. "Sure," I said and grabbed mine.

Ronan's house sat on several acres of land that butted up against the Scioto River. Between the gated backyard with the pool and the river, however, stood a grove of trees whose leaves had turned red and orange. Many had already fallen, coating the ground in that special crunchy texture only found in late fall when the forest floor frosted over. It was chilly out, but not cold enough to be uncomfortable for November, although if the temperature kept dropping like it had been, we'd have snow before Thanksgiving.

"I'm sorry about being short with you last night," Ronan said after we'd been trudging through the leaves a while.

I shrugged. "Nothing to apologize for. It'd been a long day, and I'm sure having your mother break into your house isn't easy."

"I suppose it's not really breaking in. She's right about one thing; I owe her a lot for what I have."

"Can I ask you a personal question?"

"As long as I'm not obligated to answer."

I stopped walking and turned to face him. He took a few more steps before turning around expectantly. "You're royalty. Fae royalty. Why would you walk away from that?"

Ronan sighed, his breath escaping in a puff of white. "The fae courts are complicated social machines. I was expected to behave a certain way, to stand aside and defer everything to my mother. My entire job as her son was to get married to someone politically powerful and have as many little fae children as possible. I had other ideas."

"So instead, you became a model and an amateur musician? To me, that doesn't seem like it's worth trading in a crown for."

He chuckled and turned around to keep walking deeper into the woods. "Being the son of a ruling monarch doesn't mean I'll get to be king. My mother's been in her position for thousands of years, and she'll stay there thousands more, increasing her power base as much as possible."

"Fae are immortal?"

He tilted his head in thought. "Not immortal, no. Just long-lived, I suppose. Most are, anyway. It has to do with our connection to the courts and to Faerie. The closer that connection is, the longer you live. I gave up all claim to my title and live here on Earth instead of there, so I suppose that means I won't live as long as most. Kind of makes life more worthwhile, knowing I'm not going to outlive everyone I know."

I sped up to walk beside him rather than behind. "If you gave up your titles and left, you don't owe your mother anything. She should respect your space."

He gave a derisive snort. "If only. I couldn't completely walk away. No, that would decrease her power. We had to come to a compromise. In exchange for the freedom and support I enjoy, I remain part of her court. That means I have to answer when she calls, I have to obey her orders, and I have to play the good son whenever she demands it of me."

"Why?"

"As I said, the courts are complicated social affairs. It's just how things are."

"And every fae is in a court? How many are there, and how does it get decided where you go?"

He stopped walking. "You are asking a lot of questions."

"Probably because you've been avoiding answering them. I checked the book you gave me, and it doesn't say anything about fae, courts, or dealing with royalty."

"I suppose it wouldn't," Ronan said, dusting off a tree stump. He sat on it, crossing one leg over the other and leaning back lazily. "Walter knew, but he wasn't very interested in the other world. He always said the less he knew, the better he could sleep at night. Almost anything that had to do with the fae courts, I handled or passed off to someone else when I could.

"To answer your questions, almost all fae are in a court. A few operate independently, but you'd have to be extremely powerful. Enough to be a queen in your own right, I'd think. Not even I was granted that privilege."

I crossed my arms. "People get sorted into them automatically?"

"No," he said thoughtfully. "There are only two courts. Most of us stay with the one we're born into, but there is some mobility between them. Not much, but some. On occasion, you run into someone who has enough fae blood to count who doesn't know what they are. When that happens, they get to choose which court they will swear allegiance to. There's usually a lot of contention between the courts when there's an undecided—people fighting to get them to sign on to their side. Honestly, everything devolves into childish bickering. It's not pretty. But once you have your twenty-eighth birthday, you're locked into whatever court you're currently in. For most of us, it's obvious where we belong. I don't want to imagine having to choose. Why the sudden interest?"

I considered telling him about what I'd been experiencing: the weird portals into the past, freezing the vampire, and waking up in a near-frozen room. Maybe it was magic. It might be fae magic for all I knew.

Instead, I shrugged. "Just curious."

He placed his hands on his knees. "Well then, maybe you'll indulge some of my curiosity. I've spent the last few days telling you about my family and me, yet I hardly know anything about you."

"You have my service record," I pointed out. "And you've no doubt done a background check."

"True, but all that only says so much about a person. Tell me about yourself. About the real Callie Hart."

"There's not much to me. I'm pretty boring, I promise." I shrugged and paced slowly back and forth in front of him. "I don't have much of a family aside from Sam, my roommate. My dad was never part of the picture, and my mom...she died when I was a baby. Iron poisoning, of all things. Apparently, it's really easy to overdose on it. She had an allergy to ingesting iron and didn't know."

Ronan nodded. "Even easier for fae."

"Maybe you should employ a taster in case someone crushes up iron supplements and puts them in your kale shakes." I meant it as a joke, but Ronan looked as if he were considering it. "Anyway, I spent my childhood in and out of foster homes. Signed up to be in the Army as soon as I graduated. Did my time there, came back, got my job in security, and here I am."

Ronan stood with a grunt. "Maybe it is boring. Maybe you just haven't had your adventure in life yet."

I raised an eyebrow. "My adventure?"

"Everyone has one or two. No one's life is completely boring. Well, maybe someone's is, but that's by choice. I believe everyone has something exciting waiting for them. Technically, you could count all this as your first big life adventure. It's not every day you get to save a prince and hunt assassins."

"That almost sounds like the plot to one of the books you keep in your library."

He nodded and started walking again. "It does, doesn't

it? The best stories have a seed of truth in them. Speaking of assassins, I had a thought last night. Do you think the police can match the shell casing you saw to a particular gun?"

I shook my head. "Only if it was registered to a private citizen, and if my hunch is right, this guy is not some free-lancer off the street. I think he's had military training. Someone like that is probably too smart to use a gun registered in his name. We can try that if you want to, although that means handing the evidence over to the police and letting their CSI work with it. It'd be months before we got a definitive analysis back. Crime labs are notoriously slow. It isn't like it is on TV."

Ronan frowned at me. "You don't think the person shooting at me was working on his own?"

"I think he's a hired professional. Someone with a lot of money wants you out of the way. We're better off following that angle, I think. Who benefits the most from your death?"

"No one," Ronan said, shaking his head. "That's what I can't figure out. No one should want me dead, especially anyone able to send vampires after me at a factory. If that vampire had succeeded in his attack, we'd have an all-out war on our hands. My mother would be obligated to fight until every last one of them was destroyed. Things have been tense between vampires and fae for a long time, but no one wants a war. It's bad for everyone. To try to force one would be stupid."

Maybe not, if your fortune is made when people go to war. I pictured Vaughn's smug grin in my face. How much money would he make by selling his private army to vampire higher-ups? And when the bodies started dropping in the streets, the human law enforcement agencies would want backup. He could sell consulting services to them as an expert in urban warfare. With the US ceasing many overseas military operations, his bank account had to be hurting. Maybe this was Vaughn's way of drumming up extra cash. I wouldn't put it past a vampire to go after blood money, but I couldn't make the accusation until I had irrefutable proof.

We stepped through another line of trees and were suddenly in a clearing where several wooden targets had been hung up. Ronan grinned wildly and shrugged off his coat, holding it out to me. "You want to see some magic, Callie?"

"What?"

He rolled up his sleeves. "I know you got some tossed at you last night. What you did with it was pretty impressive. I thought maybe you'd like to see what it looks like when it's not trying to hit you in the face."

Ronan turned to face the targets and unleashed a shimmering silver beam of power. It struck the closest target about the same time he let off a second shot. The second hit the target and froze it solid, just like I had with the vampire.

I sucked in a breath, watching him hit target after target, coating them in layers of ice. Magic. The word felt foreign, impossible. Yet after everything I'd learned over the last few days, maybe nothing was impossible. Magic certainly wasn't, not anymore. *What he's doing looks like what I did*. There was no denying what'd happened in that parking garage outside the club. I had done exactly what Ronan was doing, except I'd done it to a living thing.

What if I'm fae? One of those who doesn't know? It seemed unlikely, but the pieces were beginning to fit. The weird powers, the iron poisoning that'd killed my mother, my inability to fit in anywhere I went. What if the reason I hadn't been attacked in Iraq had nothing to do with me being a woman and everything to do with me being fae?

"Ronan, what happens if a vampire feeds on fae blood?" I asked suddenly.

He lowered his hand and tilted his head to the side. "Enough of it can put them in a vegetative state, or so I've heard. It's all rumors since no one's witnessed that happening for a very long time. There are also rumors that some used to do it on purpose, and that it produces a sort of relaxed euphoria."

"Which would leave them vulnerable to other predators."

"Why? What are you thinking?"

I shook my head. "Nothing." Except that I should ask Vaughn about it the next time I saw him.

That fit too, but I didn't want to go jumping to wild conclusions. There were perfectly viable normal explanations for everything, too. Until I took a harder look at my family tree, I couldn't say anything. From the sounds of it, if it did turn out I was fae, I'd have some tough decisions to make. The more time I could buy myself to learn, the better off I would be.

CHAPTER SEVENTEEN

I made it through another workday, this one without anyone trying to kill my boss or me. It was as good a day for a drink with a friend as any. By the time I got home, I was looking forward to seeing Jax. It'd been a long time since we'd met in person, and it sounded like he was doing much better. Maybe things were looking up for both of us.

The bar where we'd agreed to meet was a local hangout for the veteran crowd. It boasted lots of patriotic décor and a memorial wall and gave anyone who came in with proof of service a fifteen percent discount on drinks.

He was already sitting at the bar when I walked through the door. Jax had never been what you'd call a hottie, but the scars and skin grafts had made him look more intimidating than the guy I'd served with. I remembered his smiles and the way he turned everything into a joke. The Jax I knew could've been a comedian if he'd had a little less of a patriotic streak.

The man at the bar wasn't smiling. He sat hunched over

a drink, staring blankly at the television, where a football game played. Jax was still trying to cover his scars by turning up his collar.

I walked up to him and leaned on the bar next to him. "You know, a popped collar makes you look like an asshole."

Jax's nose twitched. "Takes one to know one."

"Aw, did you think up that comeback all on your own, private, or did your mommy help you?"

"No, but your mom did. *After* she was done screaming my name."

I gave him a punch on the shoulder. "Four months, and you greet me with weak-ass comebacks like that? Come on, Jax."

He took a long pull from the beer and rubbed his shoulder. "Damn, Hart. You've still got a mean right. You've been working on it?"

"Have to." I hopped up on vacant the barstool next to him. "I work in personal security now. Bodyguard."

"Coming up in the world, huh?"

The bartender stopped by, and I put in an order for a few more beers. "What about you? What are you doing these days?"

He shrugged. "Some freelance work. I get to travel, but the pay is hit or miss."

"You should look into what I'm doing. Lots of people need bodyguards, and the pay is much better than being in public security."

Jax didn't say anything, so I thought it would be best to change the subject. We used to talk a lot about the widows and children of the men in our unit. Jax had tried much harder than I had to keep in touch with them. It wasn't that I didn't want to talk to them, more that I didn't have anything to say. I always thought it would be better for everyone if I just let them move on, although Jax seemed to find comfort in that sort of communication.

"Have you talked to Amy or Patrice?" I asked. Those were the two widows I knew he'd connected with the most over the last few years.

Jax shook his head. "Amy moved to Montana. Haven't heard from her since. Patrice remarried about six months ago. Guess she's busy with her new life. Everyone seems to have moved on. Even you, Hart."

"Not really. I'm still the same old me."

He twisted in his seat. "Are you? I hear you're working for some rich pretty boy. You know that can be dangerous. People like that can get into awful sticky situations."

A chill ran down my spine. The way he said it, it almost sounded like a threat. How would he know who I was working for? The only person who knew was Sam, and they wouldn't have any way of contacting Jax. "How do you know about that?"

Jax shrugged. "I hear things, and I keep tabs on you."

The beers came. I passed one to Jax and frowned. "You know, if you were anyone else, I'd say that's creepy."

He pulled out his phone and showed me one of Ronan's Instagram photos. "This guy didn't get where he is by being pretty in pictures. That house he lives in? It's way too nice to buy on a model's salary, and underwear models don't need people like you protecting them, Callie. Whatever he's into, it's going to be dangerous. Trouble for you."

"You're really starting to freak me out, Jax." I leaned in

closer. "Have you been following me? How else would you know that's who I work for?"

"I just hear rumors is all. I can dig for info when I want it." He tucked his phone back into his pocket. "You should quit, Callie. I'm serious. Girl like you, with the skills you have? You can find work anywhere. Working for that guy is going to get you hurt, and I don't want to see that."

"I can take care of myself, Jax." I reached for my bottle.

Jax grabbed my wrist and I jumped. Our eyes met, and he let my arm go.

"I know you can, Callie. I'm not saying you can't. I'm just saying you don't know this guy. He's hiding something."

"Aren't we all?" I quipped and took a drink.

Jax was silent for a long time, watching the game. No, not watching it. That was a blank stare. His eyes might've been fixed on the screen, but his mind was elsewhere, thinking of everything but football.

"Do you ever think about it?" he asked after a long beat. "What happened over there, I mean?"

"Of course I do. All the time. But I can't live there, Jax. What happened is over. We were given orders to keep quiet about it."

He pounded a fist on the bar, making the nearby patrons flinch. "It's not right. I fought for this country. I've got the scars here to prove it." He gestured to his neck and chin. "But you know what I got for my trouble? A gag order and an unemployment line."

A couple of old-timers nearby grunted their approval.

I patted Jax on the shoulder. "Keep it down, man."

"It just pisses me off. All those rich assholes like the guy you're working for. What'd he do to get where he was? He didn't bleed for it. Didn't have to fight for it. I did. *We* did, and now we work for *them*. You can't tell me that doesn't make you feel at least a little dirty."

"I feel just fine about it. Ronan is a good person. Jax, maybe you don't see it, but everyone's got shit to work through. Just because you don't know what it is doesn't mean it's not there."

He grunted. "Yeah, right. Poor little rich boys and their state-of-the-art security. Glad our whole unit got murdered so you could put it on your resume."

I frowned and stood. "That's not fair. If you're going to be like this, maybe I'd better just let you drink on your own."

Jax closed his eyes and took a deep breath, slowly letting it out through pursed lips. "I'm sorry. I'm letting my temper get the best of me again. Please. I don't want you to go."

Hesitantly, I slid back onto the stool. "Tell me what I can do to help you, Jax. Are you seeing someone at the VA? They've got programs that can help you."

"I've been through them. They can't help with what I'm dealing with." Jax pushed away the beer and scratched the scarred side of his neck. "Sometimes I wonder why I'm here, you know? Why'd I make it out when they didn't? Why us? What's so special about us?"

"I don't know, maybe nothing. Sometimes, bad things just happen. Can't change that. What we *can* do is change how we react to all the shit that gets piled on us."

He laughed bitterly. "Now you sound like those VA therapists."

"Well," I replied, "maybe they're right."

Another long beat of silence passed between us. I spent it feeling guilty. Jax was right about one thing; Ronan hadn't gotten to where he was by being a model. He hadn't earned it in the traditional sense, but it wasn't like he was a bad person just because he was wealthy and lived in a nice house. As far as I could see, Ronan was a good guy with his own troubles. Yeah, maybe he could do a little more to help the local community, and he could be less self-absorbed and take fewer selfies, but he wasn't hurting anyone by living his life. He certainly wasn't hurting Jax any.

"Would it make you feel better if you met Ronan, Jax?" I asked.

Jax shook his head. "No, I'm leaving town tomorrow. Don't know if or when I'll be back. I just wanted to catch up before I did. For what it's worth, you look good. Happy, even. Better than the last time we saw each other."

"And on that note, I'm going to hit the can. Watch my drink while I go?"

He raised his beer. "You got it."

There was a line for the ladies' room, despite there being relatively few women in the bar that night. It was like magic; wherever there were women and a bathroom, there was a line, no matter how few of us there were. By the time I got back to the bar, Jax was gone. I scanned the crowd, looking for him, but he was nowhere to be found.

"You lookin' for your friend?" the bartender asked and held out a slip of paper. "Me too. He didn't settle his bill before he went AWOL."

I sighed and dug into my pocket to get my wallet. Just like Jax. *Thanks for sticking me with the bill, asshole.*

CHAPTER EIGHTEEN

The next day, I reported to work with an overnight bag in hand. The schedule said his next photoshoot was in LA, and that we'd be staying overnight rather than flying back. After the fiasco last time, that was a welcome change.

We drove to the same private hangar as before, but this time Vaughn and his people weren't waiting for us. Good, I thought, getting out of the car ahead of Ronan. At least I don't have to deal with vampires on this trip. I got on the plane ahead of Ronan and gave the interior a once-over to make sure there wasn't anyone or anything unexpected on board.

"You're taking this so seriously," Ronan said as he climbed up the stairs and onto the plane.

"That's what you hired me to do. Would you want me to half-ass this? Not when your safety and my job are on the line." I pulled down the emergency handbook on the plane and flipped it open. "Has this thing been updated in the last six months?"

The flight attendant frowned. "Federal aviation standards haven't changed. Emergency procedures are still the same."

I snapped the book closed. "What do we do in the event of some catastrophic engine failure when we're thirty thousand feet in the air?"

The flight attendant hesitated.

"Parachutes?" Ronan offered.

I glared at him. "This is a passenger jet. It's not designed to be suddenly depressurized. Open the cabin door, and you'll get sucked right out. But assuming you didn't, do you know the first thing about dropping out of a plane with a parachute?"

He shrugged and laughed. "No, not really, but I could always magic us to a feather fall when the ground gets close."

"Your body will reach terminal velocity in eight seconds," I said, ignoring his joke and sliding the book back into the plastic holder. "You'll be falling in excess of a hundred twenty miles an hour with no oxygen. Chances are high you'll pass out before we get near the ground. What then? We hit the ground, that's what."

Ronan winked at me. "Kiss me? Might wake me up."

The flight attendant giggled, and I shot her a warning glare. "I'm pretty sure we'd both be dead. If we're ever in a situation where we need to jump out of a plane, are there parachutes aboard?"

"Yes, ma'am. Enough for the entire crew plus two. That's the standard," replied the flight attendant. She brought me to the rear of the plane and showed me where they were stashed.

If I'd had my way, I would've opened each parachute and verified they were packed correctly. The last thing you want when your life relies on a working parachute is for it to deploy wrong. But we were about to take off, and I didn't have the time or space to open them to check, so I made a note on my phone to do it the next time I had a chance.

When the seatbelt light came on, I rushed to sit in the seat across from Ronan and secure my seatbelt while the captain made his introduction.

"You seem a little off today," Ronan said. "A little on edge, even. Everything okay?"

"Just doing my job. You never know when something might go wrong. Isn't it best to be overprepared?"

He leaned on his fist. "Do you ever relax? I'm starting to believe you live for work, and that's no way to be. What's the point in life if you can't have a little fun every now and again?"

"I have fun," I protested. "You're the one who's always working, flying coast to coast, avoiding assassinations. Besides, you didn't hire me to have fun. You hired me to guard you."

Ronan snorted. "Don't remind me. Let's talk about something else. Anything else."

"Okay." I gripped the armrests as the plane rumbled, climbing in altitude. That was always the worst part unless we hit turbulence. "How about this fae-vampire cold war? Give me a little history. Why hasn't there been an all-out war?"

"Well, it'd be bad for everyone, for starters. We survive because the humans don't know we're here. Imagine if they suddenly found out the couple across the street were vampires? The Neighborhood Watch would be on their front porch with pitchforks and barrels of tar. Can you imagine if they knew about fae too? The world would devolve into chaos as the humans called for us to be herded into camps, regulated out of existence, or otherwise tagged and registered like animals. It'd be worse for the vampires, who need human blood to survive. Persecution would be relentless. Safety for us comes from remaining hidden. A war would inevitably lead to a reveal the world's not ready for."

The plane leveled out, and I let out the breath I'd been holding. "What if that's exactly what someone wants?"

Ronan laughed as if it were the silliest idea he'd ever heard. "Why would anyone want that?"

I shrugged. "The point is, there are plenty of reasons for a war—more than I think you realize. There are economic reasons, for example. Anyone invested in a military force is going to see a big payday if fighting breaks out. People like Vaughn."

"Vaughn doesn't want a war. His entire job revolves around easing tensions between the fae and vampires."

"Second," I continued, "there are the political reasons for war. War provides a distraction from what's going on at home sometimes. A news story for people to focus on beyond any political scandals. It takes the heat off political figures. If you see military action spike during an election season, there's probably a reason for it."

"True," Ronan grunted. "But I'm not aware of any scandals in the vampire court, or either of ours."

"Could be one about to break, and this is the set up for a cover-up." I shrugged. "And then there's the third reason —ideological wars. Those are about imposing a certain religion or political system on an area or group of people whose way of life is different from the invading country's. Hitler's war was an ideological war, as were the invasions of the former Soviet Union, and arguably our wars in the Middle East."

"I've heard it said that was more a resource war, fighting over control of oil and that sort of thing."

"War is rarely a single-faceted event, and it's almost never about what the talking heads say it's about. If someone wants war—and we still don't know that's the case—there are probably multiple things to gain. Whatever they'd want, whoever's behind this doesn't care that the price will be paid in blood."

The flight attendant came out of her little cubby and held out a menu to each of us. "Lunch will be served on the plane."

"No, thank you." Ronan waved the menu away and dug out a plastic water bottle as well as a plastic packet of what looked like fish food. "Brought my own." He unscrewed the bottle and sprinkled the fish food into it, turning the water into thick, green goop.

I frowned and squinted at the dark green liquid. "Is that the same mix as before?"

"No, this is new. My personal trainer gave me a special mix. I'm dreading trying it, but it's supposed to be... Hey!"

Before he could finish what he was about to say, I grabbed the bottle and chugged it down. After the first gulp, I almost stopped. It tasted awful, like someone had chewed up kale and seaweed and mixed it with their saliva. Just to be on the safe side, though, I chugged the whole thing and tried to convince my stomach to keep it down. "Ugh." I held the bottle back out to him. "You're right. That's foul."

"You can keep it. I guess we're taking that whole food-tester thing seriously now?"

"Coke, please." I smacked my lips and tried to swallow the god-awful aftertaste while the flight attendant hurried to bring me a can of Coke and a straw. I ignored the straw, popped the top, and chugged the ice-cold drink. Nothing like chasing a kale smoothie with a sugary soda. "Don't eat or drink anything without me trying it first."

Ronan sighed. "I guess it's good that I wait until after the shoot. Got to look my best for it."

During the plane ride, as part of his whole argument about looking his best, Ronan decided to catch up on his beauty sleep. He snored, and it was anything but charming. I wound up putting on headphones and watching a super-hero movie.

We touched down at LAX a few hours later, and from there we took a car to the studio, which looked almost exactly like the last one. Here I'd been expecting something more similar to a movie set. Not that I knew what those looked like, but this was Los Angeles. In my mind, LA and Hollywood were the same thing.

I learned quickly that there was a lot more to the city than the movie industry. The production assistant on this shoot was a young man named Logan with spiked pink hair, a nose ring, and glasses that he probably wore for the fashion and not function. Logan was a local history buff, and more interested in imparting that history to me than assisting on set.

Much like the last photoshoot, this one revolved around putting Ronan in spring and summer attire. That meant brightly colored button-ups and jackets, jeans, shorts, and different sets of swim trunks. Unlike at the last shoot, the staff in the L.A. studio was much more laid back and less hurried. Rather than snapping hundreds of photos and choosing the best ones, the photographer spent a long time posing Ronan, moving lights around and bringing in props to get a small handful of pictures each time.

On a break, the photographer bragged to me about doing headshots for celebrities and turning down the opportunity to work on a movie. Movies, as he put it, were heartless beasts. It was easy to capture the essence of the story in a two-hour film, but doing it in a single photograph took skill.

By the time the shoot was half over, I was more exhausted than I'd been at the New York photoshoot. At least there, people had left me alone. In Los Angeles, everyone I talked to was friendly but draining to interact with. There was an air of competition, of needing to be noticed and validated I hadn't felt elsewhere. Maybe this studio and the photographer were facing stiff competition. It left me wanting to go straight to the hotel and pass out, but I still had at least two hours to kill while they finished up the photos.

It didn't help that my stomach was upset after that

disgusting smoothie. It'd started with heartburn that morphed into terrible stomach cramps. I couldn't take anything that would interfere with my ability to protect Ronan. I got through it, but it wasn't easy.

I couldn't take it anymore. While everyone was distracted by trying to set up for the second half, I snuck into a corner and went through Ronan's planner, looking at his daily schedule. Whoever had tried to shoot him knew he would be in New York. While he hadn't kept it a secret, he hadn't posted it all over social media either. The people who knew were limited to his staff and anyone involved with the New York photoshoot.

His schedule was pretty consistent. On days he didn't have to fly somewhere for work, he started his day with a trip to the gym, where he met with his personal trainer. On weekends, however, the personal trainer came to him. I hesitated, staring at the name in his appointment book. It couldn't be the same guy. He'd said he was going out of town.

Yet there was his name, written in every Saturday morning for the past six weeks—my friend, James Xavier. Jax was Ronan's personal trainer. Ronan would've told him he was going to New York because he'd have to miss hitting the gym that day. Jax also had the training necessary to make a shot like the one that had nearly taken Ronan's head off in the pizzeria.

A cold chill went through me. It's Jax, I realized, and I thought I might even know why.

"I'm starving." Ronan's voice made me jump hard enough that I dropped my phone. It clattered to the floor, landing at his feet. He picked it up and held it back out to me. "You okay? You look pale."

"Ronan, I—"

"I know what you need." He helped me to my feet. "That smoothie wasn't exactly jam-packed with calories and nutrients. You need a proper meal. Do you want steak or lobster?"

"I really think—"

"You're right. Why not both? I know just the place." He turned to walk away but paused when he realized I wasn't following.

I wanted to get it out then and there, tell Ronan it was Jax who was behind the attempts on his life, but maybe it would go down a little easier over steak and lobster. My stomach groaned, reminding me of my mostly empty stomach. Eating something light might help. "We need to talk about who's trying to kill you," was all I said.

"Over dinner," Ronan promised.

Since I knew I would be sitting with him rather than guarding him, who was I to argue if he was offering steak and lobster?

Every steak restaurant I'd been to was part of one of those national chains, but that wasn't the sort of place Ronan frequented. He took me to a place named after a celebrity chef. I felt horribly underdressed compared to all the other women in there, but no one stared. Besides, it wasn't like we were on a date. He was getting a meal, and I was there to make sure no one killed him while he ate.

Still, I had to ask when he pulled the chair out for me, "Did you take Walter out like this?"

Ronan laughed. "Walter's idea of high-end cuisine was anyplace that didn't have a drive-thru, although his bagged lunch often consisted of reheated cheeseburgers. He wasn't much for good food and not very good company. He also didn't save my life twice in one week."

"I don't want you or anyone else to get the wrong idea, is all." I thought back to his comment on the plane. It had seemed like harmless banter at first, but I had to remember that Ronan was my boss. These trips, the fancy hotel, the expensive dinners—they couldn't be the norm. We couldn't be too comfortable with each other.

He sat across from me, frowning. "I crossed a line earlier with my kissing comment, huh?"

"Maybe a little."

"Sorry. Won't happen again," he murmured and opened the menu, maybe to hide behind it.

I opened my menu but paused when a particularly bad cramp wracked my gut. I doubled over in my seat, clenching my teeth to get through the pain. *I've been through worse, I told myself.* But the cramping pain didn't subside. I closed my fingers around the tablecloth, gathering it in a fist. It'd pass, just like the others. No matter how long I tried to wait it out, however, the pain didn't fade. I couldn't keep it together.

I stood up and nearly knocked over my chair in the process.

Ronan lowered his menu. "Callie? What's wrong?"

I staggered two feet away from the table before I

dropped to my knees and vomited blood, then I collapsed to the side, too weak to move.

Ronan's chair crashed to the floor and he was at my side in an instant, lifting me off the floor and onto his lap. "We need a doctor! Someone call an ambulance!"

CHAPTER NINETEEN

I remember the trip in the ambulance in flashes. There was lots of noise. Faces I didn't recognize hovered, speaking over me instead of to me. No one would tell me what was going on or why my insides felt like they were on fire. With the lights flashing and the sirens wailing, they stuck an IV in my arm and injected me with something that made my head fuzzy. My stomach surged and I tried to vomit, but nothing came up. It felt like everything inside me was trying to claw its way out through my stomach.

I fell asleep, but it wasn't a restful sleep full of nice dreams. My mind took me through a nonsensical maze of doors and hallways. Some rooms were filled with sand or cobwebs in the corners, while others had a foreboding, ominous presence I couldn't explain. Lights flickered and doors opened on their own, beckoning me to go through them. There was a room made of candy and another where I had to wade through water up to my knees. I was fully aware that I was dreaming and kept trying to wake myself up, but I couldn't force myself into consciousness, no matter how much I screamed in the dream.

When I wasn't dreaming, I hovered at the edge of waking, aware of pressure on my arms and legs and something on my face. There were voices that belonged to people I'd never met, talking about schedules and dosages. The smell of antiseptic scorched the inside of my nose. More than anything, my stomach and throat burned like I'd swallowed hot coals.

My eyes snapped open suddenly, and I found myself staring at a paneled ceiling bathed in dim blue light. For a minute, I couldn't move. I lay there, awake, staring at the ceiling in a silent panic because my limbs wouldn't respond. Whatever sedative they'd given me must've still been wearing off. A few moments later, I was back in control of my own body. I let out a deep breath and blinked away tears from the pain of air passing over my raw throat.

Jax, I thought. *Jensen, Gormand.* The names of my former squadmates passed through my mind like water through a filter. I couldn't grab them; couldn't work out why I was thinking of them. Then it came back to me—the memory of the attack in Iraq. My head throbbed.

I reached up to touch my forehead with shaky hands, expecting to find it bandaged, but there was nothing but my own skin. *That can't be right. That thing attacked me and slammed my head into a rock.* I remembered the crunch of my helmet against stone, the sound of it cracking under the force. That shouldn't have been possible either.

I turned my head, looking around the room. It didn't

look like a VA hospital room. The little chair off to my right was upholstered and looked new. A plastic fold-out sofa was tucked against large windows, where the drapes had been pulled closed. From my bed, I could see the door to my room, shadows waiting on the other side. There was only one bed in the room. A private room? Definitely not the VA hospital, then.

I sat up, and the IV line in my arm tugged tight. I looked down and noted yellow bruising around where it went into my arm. How long had I been in the hospital?

The door slid open and Ronan backed into the room, holding a coffee cup. He stopped when he turned around and found me staring at him. "Callie! You're awake!" He immediately set the coffee cup aside and went to hug me, which felt more than a little awkward. I was still trying to remember how I'd gotten there, and I'd never been hugged by my boss before.

"I don't understand," I said as he stepped back. "What happened? Where am I?"

"Private hospital in Beverly Hills. The best in the area. I had the ambulance bring you here rather than one of the public hospitals. The care is better." He retrieved his coffee from where he'd left it near the door. "I'll get one of the nurses and let them know you're up."

"No, wait."

He hesitated by the door.

"Just give me a second to get my bearings. Why am I here? The last thing I remember is…" Images flashed through my memory, out of order. We were in Los Angeles for a photoshoot. After the photoshoot, Ronan had insisted we go to dinner, but there was something I needed to tell him. Something important. It was on the tip of my tongue, but I couldn't remember what it was.

Ronan sighed and abandoned his position near the door to sit next to me. "That health smoothie of mine you drank on the plane was laced with iron. Not enough to kill a human, but it would've been fatal to me. Callie, you saved my life. Again. If you keep this up, I'm going to have to pay you more."

I put my hands to my swimming head, trying to calm the spinning images so I could process what he'd just told me. "Iron? But…"

My mother had died of iron poisoning. The magic, the strange portals, surviving the attack in Iraq—everything came back to me. All the pieces I'd put together before flooded my brain, making me glad I was sitting down instead of standing up.

My mouth was suddenly dry. I leaned over, took Ronan's coffee from him, and gulped a mouthful of the hot liquid.

He frowned. "Are you sure that's wise? The last time you took a drink from me—"

"Ronan, I think I might be fae." I watched his face, trying to gauge his reaction, but he remained unmoved. "You're not surprised. You already knew. That was what your mother meant when she said to win me for her."

"I'm pretty sure you're only half-fae, or we would've found you a long time ago," he clarified, taking his coffee back. "Still, for a half-fae to be able to match a fae queen's magic is very rare. In fact, it's unheard of. Whoever your parents were, they must've been particularly powerful, but for the life of me, I can't think of any fae who are unaccounted for whose magic is so strong. You say your mother passed away. Someone should've noticed if such a powerful fae died."

"I think I need something stronger than coffee."

"I don't think the nurses will let you have that, not even in a private hospital."

I rolled my head to the side to frown at Ronan. "Get me out of here."

"Have to wait for you to be medically cleared. You've just been through quite an ordeal. I was worried for a while you wouldn't pull through."

I wanted to say it would take more than a little iron in a kale smoothie to kill me, but that wasn't true if I were half-fae. My fingers curled around the hem of the thermal blanket covering me. "How long have you known?"

"That you were half-fae?" Ronan shrugged. "Since that night at the factory. You have... It's difficult to explain, but when you're in your element, you have a glow that gives you away."

"In my element?" I wrinkled my nose. "What's that mean?"

"You know, when you're doing what you love. There's a part of you that likes the danger and risking yourself for other people. I saw it at the factory that night, and I've seen it several times since. When you drop your guard and let yourself enjoy things, it's obvious to anyone who looks at you that you're more than human."

I grunted. "Great, now I can glow in the dark when I take a bullet for you."

Ronan laughed and patted my arm. "I'll get the nurse to

come in and look you over. Maybe we can get you discharged sometime tomorrow and finally go home."

"Tomorrow?" I groaned and leaned back against the pillow. "Fine, I guess. As long as I don't have to eat any of that gross green Jell-O while I'm here."

Ronan fetched the nurse, who took all my vitals. She brought me water without any ice. I had to drink it and keep it down for two hours before they let me try semi-solid food, which of course meant I got to choose between sugar-free pudding and the dreaded Jell-O. Ronan was kind enough to smuggle in a Coke from one of the vending machines.

He'd flown out Ben, the other part-time security guy, and stationed him outside my door. It felt weird to be guarded when I was supposed to be the one doing the guarding, but Ronan had a point. I was in no shape to look after him. He said Ben was there for him and not me, but whenever Ronan slipped out to the cafeteria, he left Ben behind. I saw right through his scam. However, it gave me a chance to apologize to Ben for shooting him at the factory.

Rather than go back to the hotel, Ronan crashed on the uncomfortable sofa against the wall for the night. He said he felt safer there, and I wasn't in the mood to argue. My insides were still sore enough that even the pudding was too difficult to eat. The carbonated Coke was much easier, surprisingly, even if I did wind up with indigestion from it.

In the morning, they took blood to make sure my iron levels were back to normal and said if everything came back fine, I could go home.

Ronan stirred, stretched, and sat up. He looked like a

mess for once, clothes wrinkled and hair sticking up all over the place.

I grabbed my phone from the bedside table and snapped a picture. "Now, there's one worth sharing to your Instagram."

He stared at me, still bleary-eyed from sleep. "If I see that photo online, you're fired."

"I've saved your life three times. You're not going to fire me over a candid photo."

His answer was an irritated grunt as he rose for another stretch. "Do me a favor and don't get hurt anymore. These hospital sofas make for rough sleeping."

I laughed, then winced because it hurt my stomach muscles. "You want to sleep rough, you should try a military cot. Hell, they made us sleep on the ground sometimes. There were days I would've killed to have that sofa."

"You've got more tolerance for the hard life than me, I think. I'll be the first to admit my spine has been spoiled by expensive pillowtop mattresses, and I wouldn't have it any other way." He got up and went into the bathroom.

While he was gone, the nurse brought me a carton of milk and told me I had to drink the whole thing. Apparently, the proteins in milk bind to iron and help remove it from the body. At least, that was the explanation she gave me. I would've preferred another Coke, but that would have to wait.

"You still owe me a steak dinner," I said to Ronan once he got out of the bathroom.

"As long as it's not pizza. I don't think I can watch you eat that abomination you called a pizza ever again."

I was about to point out to him that after eating MREs,

just about anything was palatable when I remembered what I needed to tell him. I pushed the milk carton away. "Ronan! I know who's trying to kill you!"

He frowned and gestured to the carton. "Was the answer at the bottom of your milk carton?"

"What? No." I shook my head. "I'd just figured it out before I got sick. I meant to tell you, but everything else happened so fast, and it must've slipped my mind with all the drugs in my system. It just came back to me. Remember where you got that shake mix?"

He opened and closed his mouth, thinking about it for an extra minute. "But my personal trainer has nothing against me. He's a good guy."

"He's also a vampire."

Ronan stared at me. "No, impossible. I would've noticed."

"Not if he's hiding it from you." I pulled out my phone and opened the scheduling app. "His name is James Xavier, right?"

Ronan nodded.

"I know him as Jax, and he was the only other survivor in my unit after we were attacked by vampires."

"That's impossible," Ronan repeated, shaking his head. "What reason would he have to want to kill me?"

"I don't know yet, but it's the only explanation that makes sense." I counted the reasons on my fingers as I continued. "Jax has military training, which means he'd know how to shoot a long-range target. Not only that, but he'd be damn good at it. I also know he's been in town recently. Well, in Columbus, at least. I met him at a bar the other night."

"Wait." Ronan made a face and held up his hands. "My bodyguard and my personal trainer are hanging out in bars together?"

"It's not like that. Jax was in my unit, Ronan. I knew him from before. We were attacked by vampires in Iraq. You saw it in the report. I was not bitten, but Jax... That thing tore into him. No one thought he would survive, but what if he not only survived but became one of them?"

He crossed his arms and leaned back against the sofa, considering. "It is possible, I suppose, but I should've known."

"Can you identify a vampire on sight if he doesn't tell you he's a vampire?"

"Well, no, but—"

"You can't just look at people and know what they're capable of," I snapped. It came out a little harsher than I meant it to, but it was a lesson he needed to learn. Ronan saw the good in people and only the good. He was too trusting and carefree, and that was the reason he'd gotten into so much trouble.

Ronan lowered his head.

I sighed and rubbed the bridge of my nose, trying to ward off the oncoming headache. "I don't think Jax is a bad person, even if he is a vampire, but he's fallen on hard times. The world hasn't been kind to him since he came home. If he is a vampire, maybe it's the closest thing he's had to family in a long time. He wouldn't be after you for no reason, Ronan."

Ronan brought out his cell phone and started dialing.

"What are you doing?"

"Calling my mother."

"Why her? I thought you two had an agreement?"

"This is bigger than any agreement I have with my mother," Ronan said. "I told you, if something were to happen to me, she'd be obligated to go to war. I need to tell her what we know so she can work with the vampires to bring Jax in."

I slid out of bed and put my hand over his phone, halting his dialing. "You can't tell her, Ronan! Not yet. Please, you've got to let me talk to Jax. Reason with him. If you bring in the fae courts and the vampire higher-ups, they'll kill him."

Ronan frowned and lowered his phone. "If what you say is true, he's been trying to kill me for the last week and maybe longer."

"We're not at war yet. It doesn't have to be 'kill or be killed,' Ronan. Please. Jax is a good person in a bad situation. Please let me try."

He sighed and pressed his lips together, studying the wall behind me in thought.

I bit my lip nervously. No matter what Ronan decided, I wasn't going to let them kill Jax. If he was trying to take out Ronan, it was because someone had hired him to do it. He had said he was doing freelance work. Maybe that was his way of admitting he was working as a gun for hire. Whatever the case, my gut said Jax wasn't the mastermind behind this. Someone else was bankrolling the operation and Jax was just caught in the middle, trying to do what he thought he had to. That was why he'd warned me away from Ronan. I also thought maybe he was the one who'd taken the shot in the parking garage. If he had, that was all the proof I needed to know Jax wasn't a murderous madman who needed to die.

"I can give you forty-eight hours," Ronan told me.

I almost melted in relief.

"After that," he continued, "there won't be anything I can do. I'm obligated to report this as part of her court. I can stall for a little while, but if she confronts me directly, I have to tell her."

"I understand." I returned to my bed and retrieved my phone, opening the email app to send a hasty message. I just hoped Jax was still willing to meet. He'd said he was leaving town. Maybe if I told him it was important? No, that wouldn't be enough. I needed something that would cause him to drop everything and fly to Columbus to meet me, and there was only one thing Jax cared about enough to do that.

My fingers moved over the phone, quickly tapping out the email.

Hey, Jax. You were right about Ronan. I need your help. Can we meet same place, same time tonight?

I sent the email. I'd be pushing it for time, knowing we still had to fly east and lose a few hours to time zones, but if I got discharged before lunch, I could make it.

Jax's reply came a few minutes later, faster than I anticipated. *See you there.*

"The meeting's on," I told Ronan, lowering my phone. "But I need to be back in Columbus before six. If I'm late, he'll get spooked and walk."

Ronan pushed up from the sofa. "I'll go see if I can push the discharge paperwork along a little faster."

He left the room and I collapsed against the bed, staring at the ceiling. I'd never considered myself particularly devout, but if ever there was a time to mutter a prayer for luck, it was now.

CHAPTER TWENTY

The bar was more crowded than it had been the first time I met Jax. There wasn't a game on the television either, but they were showing the news and the weather. Typical evening television. Most everyone was drowning it out with their chatter and their beers.

Jax, however, was in his usual spot, focused on the anchor, who was covering a double homicide on the west side. I stood off to the side in the shadows near the door, watching him for a few minutes. Even knowing what'd happened to him, it was hard to accept that my friend was a vampire. I supposed that accounted for some of his difficulty integrating back into regular society. Not only did he have the normal slew of vet problems when he came back, but he'd also been grappling with a hunger for blood alongside everything else.

He must've felt so alone, I thought. Uncle Sam didn't have a transition guide for vampires. How many people had he killed to feed his hunger? How often did he need to eat? How much in control of his darker nature was he?

Jax had nearly let his temper get the best of him the last time we'd met. I'd known he was acting out of sorts, but I hadn't realized how close to a bloodbath I'd been. If I'd pushed him a little harder, would he have snapped and shown his true nature? I would have to be very careful about how I approached our conversation tonight.

I waited for a lull in the music to go over to him.

"Surprised to hear from you so soon," Jax said without turning his attention away from the television. "You seemed pretty smitten with your new job."

"Things aren't always as they appear." I slid onto the stool. Instead of ordering my normal beer, I opted for a Coke. I knew my stomach could handle that, but beer would be a gamble.

Jax lowered his bottle. "You look pale."

"I've been sick." I considered how much to tell him and then decided to throw caution to the wind. This wasn't some monster. This was Jax. I had to treat him like the man I knew was still in there somewhere. Otherwise, what was the point? I turned in my seat to face him, folding my hands in my lap. "Actually, I just got out of the hospital."

"Yeah? What for?"

"Iron poisoning."

Jax's whole body went rigid, but he still didn't look at me.

"Of course, if I hadn't been testing Ronan's food, he would've drunk that smoothie you slipped him. Since he's full fae and not half like me, he'd be dead. What happened, Jax? Did you decide the gun was too risky after you missed the first shot?"

He turned his head slowly to regard me, admitting nothing.

I decided to press the issue from a different direction. "How long have you been a vampire?"

Jax snorted. "How do you know about that?"

"Was it in Iraq?"

He turned away.

"Come on, Jax. I was there. I saw the bodies. I saw what happened to you. You shouldn't have survived. It was always a mystery how you did.

Jax's lips tipped up into an uneasy smile. "I didn't think I would, you know? Even after, when I got home, nothing was the same. The world had changed. *I'd* changed. There was nowhere I belonged. Not even the vet groups I joined helped. They didn't understand the hunger. You can't imagine what it was like, living with that."

I tried to imagine it, but he was right. I couldn't wrap my mind around what it was like to be in his shoes. Oh, I could picture it, but even with as many details as I could provide, I couldn't recreate the loneliness, the confusion, and the hunger he was talking about. "Have you killed anyone, Jax?"

"What do you think?" He picked up his beer and chugged it before dropping it heavily back on the bar. "What choice did I have? It wasn't like being a vampire came with an instruction manual. I had to figure it out for myself. I tried to resist, but you can't. If you go too long without feeding, the hunger just takes over. It makes you kill. After the first time, I figured there wasn't any point in trying to stop myself. I thought for a long time the police would find me, put me in jail. At least then, I'd get three square meals and a roof. Spent the better part of eight months hiding and looking over my shoulder. I knew how. Hiding, tracking, surviving at all costs... Even killing. We were outfitted to be what I became, except when I needed help, they told me to shut my trap and sent me home."

"Your wife, did she know?"

Jax threw his head back and let out a bitter laugh. "I doubt it. She wasn't creative enough to make that assumption. Oh, she knew I'd changed. She knew I was stronger, faster, and meaner, but she was gone long before I could show her who and what I *really* was."

"You don't have to be a killer, Jax. You can still choose a different path."

He laughed again and gestured for the bartender to bring another beer. "That's where you're wrong, Callie. This is who I am now. There's no other way for me to be. Don't you get it? I'm a predator, a killer. There's no going back for me."

I studied Jax's face and his body language. He seemed to believe what he was saying, but I didn't buy it. The Jax I knew had to be in there somewhere. All I had to do was figure out how to reach him. "What about outside the club the other night? That was you, wasn't it? In the parking garage?"

The bartender set another beer down in front of Jax and popped off the cap. He gave me a look, silently asking if I needed anything, but I shook my head, and he scurried off to the other end of the bar.

"Leave it alone, Callie," Jax said and picked up the beer to take a long pull.

I put my arm on the bar and leaned toward him. "Why

were you tailing me? Protecting me? Why warn me about Ronan if you didn't care?"

He ignored me, pretending to examine the beer bottle.

I grabbed the bottle and slammed it on the bar so hard, I was surprised it didn't break. "Stop bullshitting me, Jax! You can't save my life and then act like you don't give a shit! There's still some part of you that does give a damn about right and wrong. Drop this job against Ronan. We can talk about the rest."

He smiled at the ceiling and shook his head. "Talk it out. Why does every damn person want me to talk out my problems? As if a friendly chat with a licensed therapist somewhere is suddenly going to make my bloodlust and fangs go away." He turned to glare at me, the look so sharp I flinched. "You don't get it, Callie. People like you never will."

"People like me?"

"Sheep," Jax clarified. "You live by taking handouts from your betters, never aspiring to be anything more. Well, you can keep on taking orders from your precious pretty-boy boss if you want. I'm not going to step aside just because you've involved yourself. You know the stakes. Walk if you want, or don't. I'm done trying to help you." He stood as if to leave.

I jumped up and got in his way. "Who hired you to kill Ronan?"

Several heads turned, having heard my accusation. If I kept pushing, maybe someone would call the police, and they'd hold Jax. I could get the cops to arrest him for attempted murder. There had to be enough evidence, right? Probably not. Vaughn seemed like the sort of person who could make criminal charges go away if he greased the right palms, and I wouldn't put it past the other vampires either.

Jax tried to sidestep me. I put a hand on his chest and stood in his way.

"Move," he barked.

"You two, take it outside," the bartender shouted. "Don't make me get Security."

I ignored the bartender and kept moving into Jax's way every time he tried to step around me. He was a good head and shoulders taller than I was, and I was sure he could take me in a fight, considering he had fangs, super speed, and super strength, and I was unarmed. That didn't mean I was going to back down. I *had* to get through to him.

"Was it Vaughn Meyer?"

Jax rolled his eyes, turned quickly, and started for a side exit.

I chased after him. "It was him, wasn't it? Why? Does he want a war?"

He suddenly stopped and whirled to face me. "For the first time since I've been back, I have a family, Callie. A place where I belong. They've never asked anything of me until this, and it's the most important job they've ever given me. I'm not going to let them down just because you like your cushy new job."

"It's not about that, Jax. It's about doing what's right." I spied Security moving away from the opposite doors, pushing through the crowd and heading our way. I was running out of time. "A war will hurt everyone."

His expression hardened. "We're soldiers, Callie. War is our profession. You might've forgotten that, but I haven't."

Security reached us, two big guys with shaved heads and USMC t-shirts. "Gonna have to ask you two to leave."

"We were just going." Jax took a step forward.

I knew it was pointless, but the only thought in my head at that moment was to stop him. If I let Jax walk out of that bar, I was letting him throw his life away. Ronan would call his mother, and either the fae or the vampires would kill him. There'd be nothing more I could do to save him.

I pulled my fist back and hit him with a sucker punch right in the mouth. Jax's head jerked to the side, and I waited for Security to grab me and escort me out. For someone else to step in on his behalf. For anything to happen. For a beat, nothing did. Then Jax turned back to me, his eyes blood-red and his fangs showing for all to see.

"Holy shit," muttered some nearby patrons as they took a step back.

One of the bouncers grabbed Jax, while the other moved to take me by the arm. Jax spun on him, grabbed the big man's wrist, and yanked him forward, throwing him off balance and exposing his neck.

"No, Jax!" I shouted, but I was too late.

Jax bit into the bouncer's neck.

The bar patrons closest to us screamed and stumbled away, racing toward the exit. The bouncer who was supposed to escort me out gave up and ran for the closest door. Chaos erupted in the bar while Jax drained the life from an innocent man as if he were trying to prove his point.

Maybe he was right and he was beyond saving.

I'd failed to reach my friend. No, more than that, the

laughing, joking soldier who I'd once called my brother was gone, and in his place was a terrible monster who didn't want to be saved.

I took a step back. Every instinct in my body screamed I should run. Jax was dangerous and he'd be coming for me next, but I couldn't convince myself to move.

He dropped the bouncer's lifeless body to the floor and turned to hiss at me, blood still dripping from his fangs. I was certain he was going to attack me next, but the sound of a shotgun chambering a pair of shells echoed through the bar behind him.

"I don't know what the hell you are," spat the bartender, "but you'd best get out of my bar." He aimed the gun straight at Jax.

Jax crouched, preparing to jump the bartender, but froze when he heard sirens closing in. He hissed at me one more time before shoving me aside and running through the door into the parking lot, practically tearing the door from its hinges on his way out.

I ran into the dark parking lot after him, hoping to find him and stop him before he could hurt anyone else, but the lot was empty. Only a few cars remained. I searched between them, but there was no sign of Jax. Wherever he'd gone, I was sure I hadn't seen the last of him. He wasn't going to give up hunting Ronan.

CHAPTER TWENTY-ONE

I drove back to the loft, more pissed off than anything. The drive was a blur, and I was still on an adrenaline high when I came through the door. It was late, but not late enough that Sam would be in bed. I didn't bother trying to be quiet as I headed for the freezer in search of ice. My knuckles had turned a nice purple color and begun to throb from where they'd connected with Jax's face. Stubborn bastard had one hard head. We were out of ice, so I settled for a bag of frozen peas. Just how long had those been in our freezer anyway?

I dropped the frozen peas onto my fist and leaned against the counter with a sigh.

Sam emerged from their bedroom wearing a white tank top, lowrider jeans that left the top of their boxers visible, and a sideways ballcap. It was what I'd always called Sam's Bieber Breakdown look. "What the hell happened to you?"

"Would you believe me if I said I was in a bar fight?"

Sam looked me up and down. "You? Boring, well-behaved Callie Hart was in a bar fight?" They snorted. "I'd hate to see what the other guy looks like." Sam opened the fridge and got out a beer.

He's fine. More than fine. He's probably out there right now eating some poor bastard, I thought but didn't say it out loud. *Not only that, but he knows where I live.* I studied Sam for a minute, drinking their beer in peace. At any minute, a vampire could knock down our door, sweep into the place, and tear out Sam's throat. There'd be nothing I could do about it, especially if I wasn't there.

I lifted the peas and sighed at my bruised knuckles. They'd be a nice shade of purple in the morning and swollen. "Sam, there's something you should know. My fight at the bar was work-related."

"Your boss lets you drink on the job?"

"No, it's…" My voice trailed off as I considered how to break it to them. It might be too much to ask Sam to believe in vampires, but maybe I could make them see the danger another way. "Someone's been trying to kill Ronan. They've tried a couple of times and almost succeeded. Shot at him once and then tried poison, which I got by mistake."

"Holy shit! That's intense!" Sam lowered their beer and blinked. "Callie, are you okay?"

I shook my head. "I almost died. It was mostly luck I didn't." *And my weird genetics,* I thought but left that out too. "But this job—it's more dangerous than I thought it would be, and maybe not just for me. The people who are after Ronan know my face. They know where I live. They could come here, Sam. I don't think you're safe."

Sam dismissed it with a shrug. "There's building security here. Cameras and a doorman. We also live several floors up. Nobody's going to be climbing through our windows unless they can fly."

"These people don't have to climb through windows to get to you, Sam." I tossed the quickly defrosting bag of peas on the counter. "They could grab you off the street when you're getting a coffee or break in and wait for you to come home. They can be anywhere at any time, and you wouldn't know it."

Sam shrugged again. "So I'll get some pepper spray and have Campus Security walk me to my car. Hell, you can pick me up from class if you're so worried about me. I don't think anyone on campus would be stupid enough to pick a fight with you."

"I'm talking about professional assassins, Sam. This isn't something I would trust Campus Security to handle. You need to be somewhere safe."

"Like where?"

I considered it, tapping my fingers on the counter. They couldn't just move out. Moving took time and money, and Sam was just an art student living off of scholarship money. Affordable apartments weren't abundant in the safe areas of Columbus. Sam had other friends they could crash with, I supposed, but the vampires might find them there too. Ronan's house was a fortress, and he had more than enough room. Maybe he'd be okay with me bringing Sam there, just until things calmed down. We'd have to think of a long-term solution later.

"Let me talk to Ronan," I offered. "We'll see if he can help."

Sam's eyes doubled in size, and a smile sprouted on their face. "Do you think I could go stay there? I looked his house up online, and the pictures I saw were gorgeous. Callie, you've got to convince him to let me stay there!"

"I'll do my best. I feel bad, Sam. My work shouldn't be spilling over into your life like this. I promise it won't happen again."

"Are you kidding?" Sam squealed with big eyes and an even bigger smile. "This is the most excitement I've ever had. It'll be super-inspirational when I get back to painting. I've already decided what I'm doing for my next series: Securely Insecure. It'll be a piece illustrating your point about most security being a myth."

I sighed. Of course, that was where Sam's head was. I should've known better than to expect them to take a threat against their life seriously. Sam lived with their head in the clouds, barely in touch with how scary the world was on a good day. Sure, I'd told them about the Kloud9 thing, but they probably hadn't thought the incident would follow me home.

Sam's smile faded, and they lowered their hands. "Oh, I should be more worried, shouldn't I?"

I raised an eyebrow. "About highly trained assassins possibly ending your life? Yeah, probably. This isn't a game. I've almost died a few times already. I'd appreciate it if you'd take this more seriously, Sam."

"I'm sorry." Sam threw their arms around me and squeezed the air out of my lungs. "It's my fault all this has happened to you. I'm the one who told you to take the job. You could always go back to the boring world of corporate security, you know. I wouldn't blame you. No one would." They stepped back, their expression somber.

I forced a smile. "And give up my fat paycheck? No way."

I couldn't ever go back now, and not just because of the money. Don't get me wrong, the money and the benefits were nice, but now that I knew I was part-fae, I couldn't just walk away. Ronan was my only connection to that world. I needed to know more about who I was and where I'd come from. For the first time since I'd left Iraq, I finally felt like I had a place where I belonged and a job where I was making a real difference. I felt like I mattered, and my life had value. That was something no amount of money could buy.

My phone suddenly buzzed, and the noise made me nearly jump out of my skin. I pulled out my personal cell first, realized I'd let it die days ago, and tossed it on the counter. It took me a few minutes to dig my work cell out of my pockets. When I did, Ronan's name and number danced across the screen. "It's Ronan."

"Let it go to voicemail." Sam crossed their arms. "You've barely had any time off since you started working for him, and after what you just went through? Girl, you need to take some time to pamper yourself."

I wished I could. Aside from my bruised knuckles, the rest of me ached with the need to sleep, and my stomach was still sore from my stint in the hospital. Answering Ronan's call, however, was a matter of life and death. I couldn't ignore it, even if I wanted to.

I slid my thumb over the screen. "What's up, boss?"

He hesitated. I don't think he expected me to answer so informally, but I was too tired to play the good employee.

"Callie, I need you to come back to the house. Bring

whatever you need to get through a few days, maybe longer. I'm not sure how long this is going to take."

"Slow down for a minute, Ronan." I turned my back to Sam, although it wouldn't buy me any privacy. "What's happening? Are you okay?"

"I'm fine," he said, irritation creeping into his tone, "despite what my mother thinks. After she heard about what happened in LA, she's demanded that I come back to court because it's unsafe here. Normally, I'd tell her where she could stuff her orders, but after what happened to you, I'm starting to think maybe it's time we consolidated our people and our knowledge. Maybe we'd both be safer at court until this blows over. And who knows? Maybe you can talk some sense into her. I certainly can't."

I glanced at Sam, who was waiting impatiently for me to tell Ronan off, arms crossed. Just because Mab had called him back to court didn't mean he had to drag me along. Sam was right; I could use a few hours to pull myself together. "Are you sure you need me to go with you?"

"Of course? Why wouldn't I?"

"Well, you just said it's safer than here."

"You're the only person in the world I know I can trust right now. I certainly can't trust the people at court. I barely know them after so many years away, and my return will be seen as a threat to some of them who have climbed into the higher echelons of power. I need someone there who has my back. Can I count on you?"

I winced. The way he phrased it, there was no way I could say no without sounding like a complete bitch. He trusted me. That had to mean something.

Ronan sighed. "If you're worried about pay, I'll throw in hazard pay."

"It's not the money. It's my roommate, Sam. With everything that's going on, I'm worried Sam's not safe. Jax knows where I live, Ronan."

"Jax?" Sam whispered and swung around in front of me. "Jax is the one trying to kill you? Your old Army buddy with the big arms and the bad attitude? That's who's after you? Holy shit, Callie! That's kinda bad."

He was silent for a beat. I was sure he was going to tell me Sam was on their own. It wasn't his problem that I'd gotten my roommate involved; that much was true. We certainly couldn't haul Sam to Mab's court with us. They had no business there, and not a drop of fae blood. Who knew what Mab would do to a mortal human? Especially after the way she'd treated me.

I held my breath, waiting.

"Do they know?" Ronan asked at length. "About what's going on? Have you told them?"

"Some," I admitted. "None of the more...sensitive topics, though. Sam's okay, Ronan."

Sam folded their hands in a begging gesture. "Please, please, please, with a cherry and whipped cream on top? I promise I won't be a bother."

"Bring Sam along," Ronan said loudly since he'd heard Sam's pleading.

They did a quick celebratory dance.

"They can't come with us to court," Ronan continued, "but I need someone to stay and mind the house since I sent Thomas and Jeanie away for a few days. It's enough of a fortress that your friend should be safe if anyone invades.

We'll just have to make sure they know how to trigger the panic room."

"I can teach them." I nodded, even though Ronan couldn't see me through the phone. "Give me an hour to pack and change. I'll be there as soon as I can."

"Pack?" asked Sam once I turned around. "How much should I bring? Where are you going?"

"I can't tell you. Enough for a few days. And Sam, you might wind up missing class."

"Pfft." Sam waved a hand and made a sound reserved for children and horses. "Class, schmass. I wouldn't miss this for the world."

Sam and I went into our respective rooms to pack. I didn't know what the dress code for a fae court was, so I threw a mix of everything into the bag. Everything, that is, except for a pair of heels. I'd learned my lesson the first time. Whatever I had to do for Ronan, I'd do it in flats.

After a change of clothes and a quick splash of water on my face, I grabbed my bag and met Sam in the living room.

"You ready?" Sam asked.

I took a long look around at the familiar furniture before nodding. "Yeah, let's go."

CHAPTER TWENTY-TWO

Sam looked at Ronan with the exaggerated fangirl expression I'd seen on those Japanese cartoons they liked so much.

Ronan took it like a champ and shook hands with them as if he were used to being fawned over. "I'm glad to finally meet you, Sam. Callie has told me a lot about you."

"Really?" Sam blinked, and the glassy expression faded. "I've barely heard anything about you. Of course, she's been at work so much lately that I've hardly seen her. You should give her more time off."

I slapped my forehead and groaned.

Ronan laughed. "Callie makes her own schedule for the most part. It's just that these last few days have been difficult. I'm sure she'll give herself plenty of time off once this is all over."

"I don't know about that. Have you met Callie? She's kind of a workaholic."

"This way, Sam," I said through clenched teeth as I

pushed them toward the stairs. "I need to give you the grand tour."

Ronan smiled and waved. "Have fun, you two. Play nice, Callie."

I showed Sam the controls to trigger the protective shielding and how to open the panic room. They wanted to push the button to try it out, but activating the panic button would summon the police and the fire department. I didn't want to deal with that, so I covered the button and guided Sam safely away from it.

"What's that?" They pointed at the pile of logbooks on my desk.

"Security logs. Everyone who has a shift has to leave a summary of their shift before they clock out. It helps keep the rest of the staff up to speed. For you, it'd make for boring reading." I punched the code into the gun safe and opened it. "The code to the gun safe is on a sticky note over there, but you probably shouldn't go in unless it's an emergency. You'll be better off sticking to hitting the panic button and hiding until someone comes to get you."

"Cool." Sam wandered away while I was eying one of the new scopes Ronan had purchased. "What's this?"

I turned and found Sam rifling through a stack of USB drives on a chain. "Old security footage. Hours and hours of watching absolutely nothing happen. Shouldn't be of any interest to you." I swung the safe closed. "Ronan gave the butler and the cook a few days off. Leave some lights on at all times so they can be seen through the windows," I instructed as I led them through the top floor. "We don't want anyone to think the house is empty. Don't answer the door or the phone if it rings, though."

"What if it's a package delivery? Or what if I want to order a pizza?" They tilted their head to ogle a skylight.

"No pizza delivery, and Ronan doesn't order packages as often as you do. Any shopping you want to do will have to wait until we get back."

Sam stopped in the middle of the hall suddenly. "What if it takes weeks? Or what if you never come back?" They frowned and wrung their hands in worry.

I went back to them, gripped their shoulders, and stared them straight in the eyes. "We're coming back. I wouldn't leave you alone, Sam. Don't you trust me?"

Sam nodded.

"Then believe me when I say we'll be back. I promise."

They let out a heavy sigh and nodded again. We continued down the hall, slightly more relaxed than before.

As we reached the stairs, the strains of Ronan's violin floated up to meet us. The song he was playing sounded familiar, but I couldn't put a name to it. I swore I'd heard it before, although it was a far cry from the classical piece I'd heard him playing the first day I reported to work. This was something way more upbeat.

Sam tilted their head, listened to a few bars, let out an excited noise, and rushed down the stairs ahead of me. I called for them to wait, but it was no use. When Sam got it in their head to do something, there was no stopping them.

I didn't catch Sam until I made it to the music room. They were busy clapping and singing the lyrics to Queen's *Don't Stop Me Now*. So that was where I'd heard the song before. I hadn't recognized it on the violin.

He ended the song a verse early, much to Sam's disappointment. They clapped, more excited than anyone I'd ever seen over a violin song. "Callie, you didn't tell me he was a musician."

"Actually, I did."

"No, you said he was artsy. That's hardly the same thing." Sam turned to Ronan and did a little hop. "You're amazing."

Ronan smiled and shrugged. "I'm decent. Not great by any means. Unfortunately, I'll have to leave these behind. My mother doesn't appreciate decent music."

"I thought you said your mother insisted you learn?" I pointed out.

"True. She made me learn, but her idea of music begins and ends in the eighteenth century, as with most things, since that was her favorite century." He placed the violin back on the stand. "Callie tells me you're an artist. What sort of art?"

"Mostly abstract. Oh, and portraits. That sort of thing." Sam beamed.

I rolled my eyes and stepped farther into the room. "You're stalling, Ronan. The sooner we get this over with, the better off you'll be. Spend too long, and she'll come looking for you again."

"I know," he said with a sigh and a look around the room. "I just worry. You saw that she could be a bit... possessive. She's overreacting, but there's no talking any sense into a mother with her heart set on something. You're right, of course. We should go. The house is in good hands." He flashed Sam a smile as he collected his coat and a single duffel bag from the floor near the door.

We went to the door, and I paused. "Remember, Sam. If you need any of the house codes—"

"I know, I know. They're all upstairs in the security room in that big, ugly logbook." They rushed to give me another rib-crushing hug. "Be safe out there, will you?"

"Same to you, Sam. And don't forget, the part-timer security guards will be on a rotating schedule."

"If you need anything, don't be afraid to ask them," Ronan added.

I stepped out the door to scan for obvious problems.

Sam leaned forward to peer out into the driveway with a frown. "Don't you want someone to call you a taxi or an Uber or something?"

Ronan smiled, and when I gestured for him to come out, he did so. "No, we'll be fine. I've made arrangements for special travel. Close the door, Sam, and make sure you lock it. Anyone who needs to get in will have a key."

Sam nodded, and with one more worried glance at me, stepped back into the house and shut the door behind them.

I followed Ronan around the side of the house, wheeling my suitcase behind me.

His pleasant demeanor had faded as soon as the front door shut, and he was stomping along with a scowl fixed on his face. "When I find whoever told her what happened in Los Angeles, I'm going to make them regret it."

I shifted my grip on the suitcase handle. "If you don't want to go, why are you?"

"Because she's more than my mother," he explained, slightly exasperated. "She's my queen, and I'm beholden to her court. If she gives me a direct order, I have to obey."

"What happens if you don't?"

He stopped walking. We were a stone's throw from the

tree line, and I had no idea how far he intended to walk or to where. "If I don't show up, she'll send her knight to come fetch me, and that would be unpleasant. The knight is authorized to use any means necessary to fulfill her slightest whim." He started for the trees again, and I followed. "The only person in the whole court I hate more than Mab is her knight. Once they take their oaths, they lose all free will. All personality. They're nothing but..."

"Mannequins?"

"You have no idea how apt that description is. I'm sure you'll meet him while we're there. Don't challenge Mab's knight, Callie. You're clever, strong, and resourceful, but he's relentless, devious, and brutal. He'd do things you couldn't even conceive of to carry out his orders."

He sounded evil, but I was dealing with a society that was totally different from anything I'd ever experienced. In the right context, people saw soldiers in much the same light, I supposed. I'd met more than one person in my time who demonized the men and women who went overseas as murderers or characterized us all as headcases. Not everyone who served came back broken.

I suspected even Jax would have turned out fine if the civilian world hadn't mistreated him when he got back. It wasn't any one thing that'd broken him. It was the way his family, his government, his friends had all let him down over time. I'd let him down too. I should've paid more attention to Jax and the way he was acting when we got back, but I thought the best thing for him at the time was the space to work it out on his own.

Ronan stopped so suddenly I almost bumped into him. We'd reached the clearing where he was hitting targets the other day. Rather than throw more spells at targets, however, he dropped his bag on the ground and pulled a ring from his pocket. The stone in the silver ring had to be one of the biggest, brightest blue topazes I'd ever seen, not that I'd seen that many. It'd been designed to look like a rosebud, with the ring bearing several leaves. Ronan slid it on, wincing like it hurt. I didn't see why until he lifted his hand palm-up and several drops of blood hit the ground.

Magic swirled up like a storm cloud in front of him, an icy wind tossing aside the leaves covering the forest floor. Lightning flashed, but not above us; it was in the clearing with us. The electric current made our hair stand on end. Ronan made a subtle motion with his hands and the electrical energy sped to a point on the other side of the clearing, where it exploded in a flash of light.

I turned away, shielding my face. When I looked back, a glowing blue portal stood in the center of the clearing, with ice rimming the edge. The center was an endless black hole.

Ronan removed the ring from his finger and shook it. "I hate doing that." He dropped the ring into his pocket before bending over to pick up his bag, which he slung over his shoulder. "Well, let's get this over with."

"Wait."

He paused and turned around, his head tilted slightly to one side as if to ask a question.

"You've got no idea what's waiting on the other side of that thing." I gestured to the portal. "I should go through first."

"I think in this case, it would be better if you didn't," Ronan said with a frown. "Fae aren't trusting types. Aside from Mab and me, no one knows who you are. With tensions on the rise, the guards might err on the side of caution. I don't want you to get hurt."

I cringed. "You're telling me they might kill me just for walking through?"

"Not if we go through together." Ronan held out his hand.

I picked up my suitcase and took Ronan's hand. He closed his fingers around mine and offered a reassuring smile as we approached the portal. The air around it smelled like cinnamon, an odd smell to pick up out in the woods. Although I knew it was silly, I held my breath and closed my eyes as we stepped through.

It felt like walking through liquid plastic. The strange black goo stuck everywhere. When I tried to pull away, it clung to me, dragging me farther in. For a moment, I panicked and tried harder to pull away. I tugged on Ronan's hand, but he held firm. I opened my mouth to shout a warning that something was wrong, but the black goop raced into my mouth, speeding down my throat to coat my lungs like water.

Ronan's fingers slipped from mine.

I tumbled through the other side, gasping, and fell to my knees. To my surprise, the strange goo didn't drip from my hair or clothes. I was dry, despite the way the portal had felt. One thing I wasn't was warm. The other side of that portal was freezing, practically subzero. I'd dressed for cold, but not that cold.

Ronan helped me to my feet, mumbling an apology. "Sorry. I forgot how scary it was the first time. You'll get used to it."

"Get used to it?" I jerked my hand away from him. "I don't think I want to! That was..."

My voice trailed off as I got a look at the winter wonderland around us. A thin layer of ice coated everything. Although the air was freezing, the sun shone brightly in the clear sky above. Icy blocks formed three walls around us as well as the floor, but the room we'd stepped into had only a partial ceiling that rose toward the center in sharp spikes.

I paced forward a few steps to the center of the room. "Are we in some sort of prison cell?"

"This is the old palace," Ronan explained. "I didn't want to just drop into the throne room and make a big deal."

Metal clanked, and heavy footsteps closed on our location. A moment later, a whole company of guards in shining silver plate armor marched into the room and drew their swords, pointing them at me.

Ronan stepped in front of me and shoved one of the swords away. "What's the meaning of this? She's my guest, here under my protection!"

No one moved.

Ronan dared to step closer, seizing the sword out of one of the guards' hands. "I asked you a question!"

"Uh, Ronan?" I pointed to the doorway.

A new creature had entered the room, this one tall, lanky, and dressed in deep blue armor. He didn't walk so much as spring out of the ice, reforming closer with every step, eternally connected to the frozen world. His face was hidden behind an eyeless mask. The sword he carried on his back was easily large enough to take several heads at once.

Ronan stepped away from the guards and stood in the creature's way. "Sir Knight, you have no business here. We are Her Majesty's guests."

The knight's answer was a whisper I couldn't make out.

Ronan gave me an apologetic look. "Go with them, Callie. Don't fight them."

One of the guards grabbed my arm. "What the hell's going on?" When a second guard took hold of my other arm, I reached for the magic that had let me freeze the vampire solid, but it didn't respond. "Ronan! What's happening?"

He lowered his head and stepped back as they dragged me toward the exit. "I'm sorry. I didn't know. I'll fix this, Callie. I swear."

The knight didn't turn, but somehow his body flipped and he led the guards out of the room, dragging me with them.

CHAPTER TWENTY-THREE

I thought they'd haul me off to a freezing dungeon somewhere or drop me on a chopping block. For all I knew, I'd broken some fae law I didn't know existed. The dark figure Ronan had addressed as "Sir Knight" never spoke. He never even looked at me as they half-dragged, half-escorted me through endless icy hallways.

The farther we went, the wider the hallways became. Tables, also made of ice, lined the walls, bearing vases full of frost-covered roses. More guards stood on either side of a huge set of double doors. The doors creaked as they pulled them open. I'd given up trying to walk. Might as well let them carry me and save my energy. I certainly wasn't getting away.

The room beyond was twice as big as any room I'd ever seen, with a domed ceiling depicting a great battle between soldiers made of ice on one side and a burning forest on the other. At the head of the ice army rode Mab on an armored white horse, while a dark-haired queen on a winged horse led the charge on the other side. Icy white columns stretched from floor to ceiling.

When I saw Mab waiting at the other end of the room, perched in her throne, I renewed my fight, pulling away from the guards who held me. "I should've known it was you."

"Quiet, prisoner." Someone pulled my feet out from under me.

I hit the ice floor face-first. Pain spread through my chest and shoulders, but I pushed through it to lift myself to my knees. I would've stood back up, but the guards held me down.

"You should count yourself lucky I've only had you brought before me," Mab said, raising her sharp chin. "You attacked me in my son's home, and then you were foolish enough to come into my domain? You, an undecided? A *rogue*?"

"First of all, *you* attacked *me*. You don't get to be pissy because I defended myself. I was just doing my job, which your son hired me to do. If you don't want to have your magic thrown back at you, don't break into people's houses and attack their bodyguards in the dark!"

Mab shifted in her throne. "Yes, well…" She cleared her throat. "That is another matter and not why you've been brought before me today. Undecided fae are not permitted to wander freely through the kingdom as they see fit." She waved a hand.

"Are you serious?" I raised my eyebrows and regarded the queen doubtfully. "You want me to pick a side right now? I don't have time for this."

The queen started to say something else, but a commotion at the doors made her pause. I turned around.

Ronan shoved one of the guards out of the way and stormed to the middle of the throne room, fists clenched. "Release her immediately!"

Mab's face sprouted a vicious smile. "Welcome back, son."

He ignored her and pointed emphatically to the floor. "Let her go, Mother. Now."

"Unfortunately, you're not in a position to make demands, Ronan. You know the law." She gestured to me. "Miss Hart cannot be allowed to wander aimlessly as an undeclared fae. However, if she were to pledge herself to our court..."

"You couldn't have picked a worse time to pull this stunt." I took a step forward but stopped when I felt the faceless knight's gaze. I couldn't see his eyes, but I could swear he was staring straight at me. I swallowed and continued, addressing Queen Mab. "Look, I understand there are laws and rules, but I didn't even know I was part-fae until yesterday. You can't expect me to just pick a side. I don't know anything about the other court. I have the right to do a little research, at least."

"Out of the question." Mab sliced her hand decisively through the air. "I will not allow you to work for my son if you even consider my sister's court!"

"It's not up to you!" Ronan growled. "You've overstepped."

Mab pushed herself up from her throne, her eyes darkening. Her voice boomed like thunder through the throne room. "I am the queen! You are my subject, and you will obey!"

"You're a tyrant," Ronan snapped back. "And I wouldn't blame her for joining Titania."

The queen puffed her cheeks out, gathered her skirt, and stormed down from the platform where the throne sat. "Why, you ungrateful brat! I've given you everything! *Everything!* And this is how you repay me?" She stopped in front of Ronan and drew herself up so she was a head taller. "I'm beginning to wish I'd never had a son!"

"The feeling is mutual."

"Enough!" I shouted.

They stopped arguing long enough to face me.

I massaged my throbbing temples. "Can you two just shut up and get along for a few seconds so we can focus on what's important? There's a bad guy out there who wants to kill Ronan. Your Majesty, surely you can see this is a bad time to force my hand. We came here because you called Ronan. I didn't come to invade your court. I came because it's my job to protect your son. You care about his well-being, don't you?"

She bristled. "Of course I do. Why do you think I called him back here? Why do you think I'm gathering my armies for war?"

"War?" Ronan gave her a shocked look.

"They're trying to kill you," said Mab, cupping Ronan's cheek. "This has gone on long enough. It's time they felt the full force of my court. We will wipe them from the Earth, and then you'll be safe."

I glanced at the knight and stepped away from my

captors. No one chased me. "That's a little extreme, considering you don't even know if the assassin is acting on their orders or if he's on his own."

Mab regarded me coldly and turned away from Ronan. "I don't need to know that. I know the assassin is a vampire. You confirmed it, according to Ronan. Even if the others aren't involved, they've done nothing to stop it."

"What about Vaughn's investigation?"

"If you call that an investigation." She rolled her eyes. "He's produced nothing, and he's had a whole team working on the case. You've collected more evidence and gotten farther than anyone else. Based on your conclusions and their inaction, it would appear the vampires want war. And if war is what they want, we shall give it to them." Mab paced back to her throne.

"I don't believe all the vampires are involved." It was true, but only by splitting hairs. I didn't know every single vampire in the world, and it was possible there were some out there who didn't want a war with the fae. I was convinced Vaughn was involved somehow, even if I couldn't prove it, but what if I could prove Jax's mission wasn't sanctioned, or at least cast reasonable doubt on it? That might be enough to deter the queen from going to war.

"It doesn't matter if they're all involved." Mab lowered herself onto the throne. "I have to put a stop to this, or I'll be seen as weak."

"What if I can prove it?" I took a step toward the throne but stopped when the knight's hand went to the hilt of his sword.

Mab leaned on her fist. "Go on."

"Jax has had a hard time. He's a traumatized soldier who hasn't readjusted to civilian life. I knew him in the Army. We served together. It's possible he's targeting Ronan because of his proximity to me."

Ronan frowned. "Why would he do that?"

"I don't know, some protective instinct? He's sick, Ronan. There's no reason to go to war because one vampire is acting erratically. If the vampires really wanted Ronan dead—all the vampires—they would've launched a larger offensive by now. Instead, there's one person making all the moves. Where's his backup? Why haven't they used someone else when he failed if they were so hell-bent on starting a war?"

"You raise good questions, girl." Mab tapped her chin.

I chanced another step closer to the throne. "If I can prove Jax is acting on his own, will you call off your armies?"

The queen turned her attention to Ronan. "You know her better than I do. Tell me, son, do you trust this woman?"

Ronan met my eyes and nodded. "Callie wouldn't lie. She's saved my life three times, nearly at the cost of her own. Her loyalty isn't in question. Her cooking skills, however..."

I raised an eyebrow. "Seriously? I'm trying to stop a war here, and you're going to complain about my cooking? Which you've never had, by the way. Since when was that part of my job description?"

"Since you decided you're going to start tasting all my food."

"First thing I'm going to make you is a knuckle sandwich," I grumbled. "What year is this, 1950?"

Mab put a hand to her ear. "What's that?"

"Nothing."

She narrowed her eyes but chose not to pursue it and focused on the more important problem. "If you can prove beyond a shadow of a doubt that your friend is working alone with no support from the vampire aristocracy, and if the attempts on my son's life cease, I will not launch an attack. There will be no war against the vampires."

"Yes! Score one for the home team." I pumped my arm in celebration.

"But," continued the queen.

Great. There was always a but, wasn't there?

She steepled her fingers and tapped them together. "You only have twenty-four hours."

My jaw dropped. "Twenty-four hours? That's not nearly enough time!"

Mab smiled. "I'm afraid that's all the time I have to give. If you can't do the job in the allotted amount of time, I will have no choice but to proceed as planned."

"But—"

She cut me off with a wave of her hand. "In addition, if you succeed, I will give you thirty days to decide to join my court. You may use that thirty days however you choose. However, bear in mind that I will not allow you to continue to work for my son if you choose to join my sister's court. That might not sound fair, but you must acknowledge that such a choice would create a conflict of interest. I simply cannot allow it."

Stopping Jax inside twenty-four hours seemed impossible, but it was the only option I had. If I failed, not only would the fae and the vampires go to war, but I would also lose my chance to make an informed decision about which fae court to join. Accepting Mab's offer was the only real option, especially if I wanted one more chance to try to talk some sense into Jax.

"Agreed," I said, stepping forward. "But I have to return to Earth, and I need Ronan to come with me."

The queen let out an exasperated gasp. "Whatever for? You must acknowledge that he is safer here than he is there, even with you by his side. You can't protect him from everyone all the time."

I exchanged glances with Ronan. "No, but if I want Jax to show himself, I will need Ronan there. He's not going to come out to talk to me." *I already ruined that chance.*

Mab wrinkled her nose. "You need to use my son as bait?"

"I promised you no harm will come to him. If it looks like the situation is getting out of control at any time, he can open a portal and come straight back here." I bit my lip, waiting for Mab's response. If she turned me down, I didn't know what I would do. After the fight at the bar, Jax had probably gone to ground. The only way to get him to come out now would be to give him a target he couldn't resist.

"She's right," Ronan said, stepping forward. "And I trust Callie with my life. If you want to catch the assassin, this is the best way."

The queen gave a loud sigh and waved her hand dismissively. "Very well, have it your way. But if something happens to Ronan in your care, know that I will hunt you to the ends of the earth and beyond. And when I catch you, and I will, our interactions will redefine the word agony. Have I made myself clear, Miss Hart?"

I nodded. "Crystal."

"Then go. You have twenty-four hours, beginning now."

CHAPTER TWENTY-FOUR

I stood in front of the glowing portal that would take me back to Earth, waiting for Ronan to wrap things up. I tapped my foot impatiently on the ice, and I glanced at my watch twice before I realized it wasn't working. *Come on, Ronan. Where the hell are you?* I only had twenty-four hours to catch Jax and prove to the queen that the vampire aristocracy hadn't been in on hiring him, and he'd stopped to chat?

"There you are," I said as Ronan came jogging up to me. "Where've you been?"

He held a manila folder out to me. "I thought you should have this."

I took the folder and opened it. Inside was my entire service record, redacted interview and all. "I thought the last copy of this had been destroyed. Where'd you get this?"

Ronan rubbed the back of his head. "Vaughn Meyer. He does all my background checks for me. He pulled some strings high up at the Pentagon. I didn't realize he'd gone through all the trouble until recently. The file he gave me was incomplete. A lot was blacked out, but I got my mother to give me the full file. I didn't know the full extent of what happened to you in Iraq until I read that."

"But you read parts of my file to me during—"

"Just the parts Vaughn had given me," he clarified. "When you asked if I had a security clearance, I wasn't honest with you. I meant that I had clearance here, in my mother's court. Vaughn is my connection to getting classified information when I want it."

"Which means Vaughn has access to classified information whenever *he* wants it." I flipped the folder closed and tucked it into my coat. "Why would he have those connections? I know Meyer Securities has government contracts, but they wouldn't usually get access to this kind of information just because they requested it. There are laws in place to keep that from happening."

"Apparently, Vaughn has ways to circumvent those laws."

That was worrying. If Vaughn had ways of getting around the laws and knew people high up in the government, he was going to be difficult to deal with. I hoped I was wrong about him hiring Jax. Ronan didn't say it, but the implication was there. *He must've figured it out too*, I thought. He must have realized Vaughn was the only one who had something to gain if the vampires and the fae went to war. But was he? I knew nothing about the summer court. I filed that thought for later when Ronan kept talking.

"Maybe we can get Jax's file too," Ronan suggested. "I can call Vaughn. It might help."

"No thanks," I said, turning around to face the portal. "I'd rather not deal with Vaughn anymore unless I have to."

We stepped through the portal. Ronan might've thought it would be easier the second time, and maybe it was, but I still felt like I was drowning in goo. Whatever the portal was made of, it felt like walking through thick, melted plastic. I came out the other side gasping for air and choking.

"Are you okay?" Ronan patted my back as I bent over coughing.

"Yeah. Just remind me next time to hold my breath."

"There won't be a next time if I can help it," Ronan said, helping me up.

I frowned at him. "What do you mean? Don't you want me to join your mother's court?"

"You saw how she was. Is that the kind of court you want to belong to?"

We started walking at a slow but steady pace. I wanted to move faster, but I needed to reserve my energy. Chances were good that my confrontation with Jax would end in some sort of fight. If I wanted to have a chance at taking down a vampire, I needed to be in peak physical condition.

"No," I said hesitantly. "But do I have a choice? I mean, I have to choose one or the other, right? There are only two options?"

Ronan nodded. "Either Mab's court or Titania's. Winter or summer."

"What about being independent?"

Ronan stopped walking and turned to face me. "I'm sorry, I thought I made that clear the last time we talked. Neither Mab nor Titania will allow you to remain independent. You need their permission. Permission from both of them. That means they'd have to agree, and they haven't agreed on anything since the beginning of time."

"I thought you said that there were independent fae, even if they were few and far between."

Ronan started walking again, albeit slower. "That is true. However, all the independent fae I know of either predate Mab and Titania, or they are powerful enough to run a court in their own right but choose not to."

"But I am pretty powerful," I said practically running to keep up with him. "You said so yourself. Not just anyone could bat Mab's spell back at her like I did. There has to be a way."

He waved his hand, dismissing the thought. "We can talk about that later. You have thirty days to decide. Right now, we should probably come up with a plan. How do you intend to get Jax to show himself?"

Despite what I had told Mab, I wasn't comfortable using Ronan as bait to draw Jax out. Maybe we could find a look-alike, or Ronan had a spell that could create an illusion.

When I asked him about it, he laughed. "Magic doesn't work like that, Callie. I can't just make a copy of myself. Some days I wish I could, though." He stopped me again just before we got to the house. "I know you told my mother you didn't think the other vampires were behind Jax's assassination attempts, but that's not true, is it?"

I turned away, not wanting to face him as I admitted I had lied, even if it was a lie by omission.

"You think Vaughn is involved," he continued.

I nodded. "Not only do I think he is supplying Jax with

the weapons and ammunition he needs to shoot you, but I think this whole thing was Vaughn's idea. He set it all up. He recruited Jax, armed him, and set him up as your personal trainer, and when he was called on to investigate, intentionally obstructed that investigation. Think about it, Ronan. Vaughn is one who does your background checks. How could Jax have slipped through? When Vaughn ran the background check on Jax, he would've known Jax had a military service record. Did he share that with you?"

Ronan shook his head.

"The question is, why?"

"Greed?" Ronan shrugged.

"Maybe," I agreed. "But he's already filthy-rich from his Department of Defense contracts. He is the CEO of a Fortune Five Hundred company. What does a guy like Vaughn Meyer gain from a war between his people and yours? It feels like it should be something more substantial than money. There are easier ways for someone who's already rich to amass more wealth. Easier ways than sacrificing hundreds, if not thousands of lives." I pulled up the control app on my phone. "I hope I'm wrong."

"And if you're not? What will you tell Mab? Will you tell her the truth if it leads to war?"

I considered the question, my hand resting on the knob. If I was right and I told Mab, I would be sending people to their deaths. Did I want their blood on my hands? Did I want to be responsible? It wasn't an easy choice to make: to tell the truth, or save lives. What kind of crazy, messed up world did I live in for the two to be mutually exclusive? Besides, I wasn't sure Vaughn was the only choice for the villain of this piece. There was still the summer court, although I didn't immediately see what they had to gain except to weaken the winter court.

"I will do everything in my power to prevent a war," I said. It wasn't a complete answer, but it was one I could live with.

I pushed open the door, only to find myself face to face with the barrel of a gun.

"Reach for the sky, bloodsucker!" Sam shouted and pulled the trigger.

I yelped as a blast of icy water sprayed me in the face. "Sam! Cut it out! What the hell?" I shook water from my clothes.

"Oh, sorry! I heard voices and the door rattled...and you two said you wouldn't be back for a long time, so I thought..." Sam pulled a hand towel down from where it hung near the stove and held it out to me. "I'm sorry, Callie."

"A squirt gun?" Ronan confiscated Sam's weapon before they could do any more damage.

"I found it in the pantry when I went to find something to eat. It's full of holy water," Sam chirped.

"Holy water?" I lowered the towel. "Wait a minute..."

Sam nodded.

Ronan chuckled and handed the squirt gun back to them. "You thought we were vampires."

"Ronan, I swear, I didn't tell Sam about vampires or fae or anything,"

He held up a hand and shook his head as if it wasn't a big deal that my roommate had somehow figured out there were supernatural monsters in the world.

I turned to Sam. "How did you find out?"

They gave me a guilty look and then stared at their sneakers. "I might have spent the last few hours watching a bunch of footage and reading your security logs."

I slapped myself in the face. Of course, that was the first thing Sam would do. I'd written every detail in the logs, not anticipating needing to bring them into the house. Anyone who might see the logbooks and security footage already knew about vampires and fae.

I sighed and held out my hand. Sam slapped the water gun into my waiting palm. "You know you can't just make holy water, right? There's a process. And it doesn't work on vampires...does it?" I looked at Ronan.

"It does not," he confirmed. "Although a spray of ice-cold water in the face is sure to stop any intruder in their tracks, at least for a moment. I admire your ingenuity, Sam."

Sam beamed, but their smile quickly faded. "Oh, and um, sorry about the smudges on the pages. They might or might not be the Death by Chocolate ice cream from your freezer."

I put both the water gun and the towel on the counter. Smudges on the security log were the least of my worries. I was running out of time to come up with a plan that would help me catch Jax and stop the fae and vampires from going to war with each other, and Jax wasn't going to take my calls.

My phone buzzed in my pocket, and I pulled it out. It was a reminder that Ronan was supposed to meet someone for lunch.

Ronan fished his phone out of his pocket at the same time. "Well, I guess I'm canceling my lunch date."

"Wait a minute." I waved my phone at him. "Did you give one of these to Jax?"

He shrugged. "I give everyone on my staff a phone, so they can have access to my schedule."

"Can I work for you?" Sam asked.

"Not now. I think I've figured out how to get him. Sam, you know people in the performance arts. Do you think you could help us book a venue?"

They blinked. "Sure. What kind of performance?"

"Musical," I said. "Whatever it costs, find us somewhere tonight."

"I know the perfect place." Sam's smile widened as they scrolled through their phone.

CHAPTER TWENTY-FIVE

I lowered the phone. "Okay, Ronan's schedule has been updated to reflect the concert. Now all we need to do is get him there in time and make sure everything goes as planned."

Ronan snapped his violin case closed. "Are you sure this will work? What if he doesn't have his phone anymore? Or he suspects a trap? What then?"

I didn't know how to answer him. This was my one shot. If it didn't work, I was out of ideas, but I couldn't tell him that. "It will work," I said, tapping the phone on my open palm. *It has to.*

Sam came out of the back of the house, tucking their hands into their back pockets. "Everything is squared away with the Palace Theater. The venue is yours for a private show for the rest of the evening. Are you sure you don't want Columbus PD on standby?"

I shook my head. "Human cops will just get in the way. This is something we have to handle on our own. Besides, can you imagine explaining vampires, fae, and magic to a Columbus cop?"

Sam snorted. "Good point."

Ronan picked up his violin case. "Are you sure you want to do this, Callie? Jax was your friend. This isn't going to end well. You might even have to kill him."

That was a point I had already considered. Jax was beyond a friend, more like a brother. We had served together, shed blood together, and watched our friends die together. That was a bond that couldn't be bought, a respect that could only be earned between soldiers. If I fought my brother-in-arms, was I betraying that bond? Was I betraying *him*?

I took a deep breath. "You hired me to protect you, Ronan, and that's what I'm going to do. The Jax who is trying to kill you is not the Jax I served with in Iraq. This new Jax may wear his face, might have his voice, and might even have his memories, but it's not him. The Jax I knew died the day he was attacked in Iraq.

Ronan blinked, hesitating. "I believe you."

That makes one of us, I thought. "Come on. We'd better get to the car, or we'll be late."

Sam put their arms around me. For once, I was ready to have the air squeezed out of my lungs. "Good luck. Oops, sorry. It's bad luck to say good luck to a performer, isn't it?" They grinned. "Break a leg, Ronan!"

"Please don't. I don't want to have to explain that to your mother." I escorted Ronan from the house to the car, scanning the area as I walked. The chances that Jax would be nearby were slim to none, but I could not be too careful. He knew where Ronan lived, and after his last failure, he'd be desperate to perform. I hoped that meant he was motivated to show up at the Palace Theater. I didn't think his vampire employer would tolerate half measures.

The drive across town was nerve-wracking. I couldn't help but track the cars outside the window, wondering if Jax was in one of them. In my mind, I pictured our confrontation. If I was careful, maybe I could just disable him. Shoot him in the leg or the arm, or somewhere else nonfatal. Even as I thought that I knew it wouldn't work. Jax would keep coming after Ronan. The only way to stop him was to put him down.

"I always wanted to play the Palace Theater," Ronan remarked.

I turned away from the window and found him gripping his violin case hard enough that his knuckles had turned white. Although his face didn't betray it, he was nervous. Maybe as nervous as I was, and for a good reason: his life was on the line.

I flashed him my best reassuring smile. "Sorry it couldn't be a show with an audience."

Ronan chuckled. "Well, maybe one day. Then again, I have people looking at me all day, every day. It's kind of nice, knowing I can perform without an audience for once, even if it is only the violin."

"You say that like the violin is easy or something."

He shrugged. "It is for me. I've been playing almost all my life. If I'd had more time to prepare, I would've liked to do a one-man show."

"You mean, like those guys who play the kazoo and the piano and tap a drum with their foot?" I tried to imagine

Ronan doing an act like that and wound up snickering because it looked so silly in my mind's eye.

"Everybody's a critic!" Ronan finally let go of his violin case and crossed his arms. "Okay, Miss Music Critic, what kind of music do *you* like?"

"You know, the normal stuff: Metallica, AC/DC, The Chili Peppers. Anything that doesn't sound good played on a violin."

Ronan laughed at that. "Now that's where you're wrong. It's a complete misconception that you can't play metal on a violin."

"I didn't say you couldn't play it, just that it wouldn't sound good."

He leaned forward. "How'd you like to make a bet? I'll bet you a steak dinner that I can play one song from each of those bands and make it sound good."

"You already owe me a steak dinner for saving your life from the awful iron smoothie." I glanced into the rearview mirror. Was that black Suburban following us, or was I being paranoid?

Ronan suddenly put his hand over mine. "Thank you, Callie."

"For what?"

"For everything. Not just for saving my life. I know you think that's part of your job, but not everyone would do that. Not only for that, but for supporting me with my mother. For being there in general. I don't know where I'd be without you."

My cheeks warmed, and I pulled my hand away. "You can make up for it by not dying today. I'd hate for you to ruin my perfect record."

"You know, it's okay if this doesn't work. No one is going to hold it against you if he doesn't show."

I'll hold it against me, I thought. *And probably Queen Mab too. She won't be happy if anything happens to you.* Actually, that was an understatement. She'd probably skin me alive or worse. Who knew what sorts of punishments that creepy queen was into?

"It will work." I leaned forward to address the driver. "Can we take the next exit?"

"Exit for the Palace Theater isn't for another few miles," he said.

"I know that. A black Chevy Suburban has been behind us for a few more miles than I'd like. I want to make sure it's not tailing us. You can get right back on the highway if I'm wrong."

Ronan frowned and twisted in his seat to look out the back window.

I grabbed his arm. "Don't do that."

"Why not?"

"Because if they are following us, we don't want to tip them off that we know. Nobody would be following us right now for a good reason. Just in case, you should settle into the seat and try to keep your head down." I didn't think anyone would be stupid enough to shoot at us on the highway, but if Jax was getting desperate, there was no telling how far he'd go.

The exit took us downtown, where traffic was thick. Buses crowded the right-hand lane, and busy people hurried on sidewalks, checking their watches to make sure they could make their last meeting of the day. At first, I didn't think the Suburban had followed us, but then I spied it in the mirror two cars back. *That doesn't mean it's following us,* I told myself. *They could just be going downtown. Lots of people go downtown, especially at this time of day.*

As we sat at the light, I came up with every excuse in the book for why that black SUV had been in our rearview mirror almost since we'd pulled out of Ronan's driveway. Even if they were following us, that was no proof of sinister intentions. Ronan was a celebrity of sorts. Maybe he'd attracted some paparazzi. Maybe he had a crazy fan. The longer we sat at the light, however, the more sure I became that it was Jax or someone working with him.

"Take a left," I told the driver.

"But I'm in the right turn lane!"

"If Callie says take a left, Vernon, you take a damn left!" Ronan ordered.

The light turned green, and the tires on our sedan screeched as the driver hit the gas and spun the wheel to the left, cutting off traffic. Horns blared and brakes squealed. Angry drivers waved fists and fingers, but we managed to make a left turn without causing a wreck.

I spun in my seat and watched as the Suburban pulled out of traffic into the oncoming lane and sped after us. The car came close enough I was finally able to see through the windshield and make out the details of the driver's face. It wasn't Jax, but I had seen him before. It was one of Vaughn's henchmen. There was no doubt in my mind that we were being followed.

"Drive faster!" I shouted to the driver.

He stepped on the gas and the car lurched forward. My back pressed against the seat with the sudden increase in speed. We jerked into the shared turn lane to avoid traffic, then back into our lane. I thought I was going to be sick as the driver wove in and out of traffic, trying to lose the Suburban, but he handled the car like a pro.

We sped up by the convention center, and the driver jerked the wheel to the left. Our back tires screeched as they slid across the pavement, and the car sailed onto Nationwide Boulevard. After another hard left, we slid into a parking garage and bounced over a speedbump that sent me sailing towards the ceiling. With all the skill of a professional stunt driver, Vernon slid the car into a tiny parking space between two big trucks and immediately shut off the engine.

I pulled Ronan down so that we would not be visible from the narrow aisle. We waited in silence, practically holding our breath as we waited for the Suburban to pass us. The dull roar of an engine crawled by our hiding spot, and I was sure the jig was up. There was no way he wouldn't spot us. But the car inched by, and the driver gave the all-clear.

"What was all that?" Ronan asked, sitting up. "Was it Jax?"

The driver pulled the car out of our hiding spot and headed for the exit.

I shook my head. "It was one of the vampires from before. One I saw standing with Vaughn at the airport."

"Why would Vaughn need to have us followed?"

"Probably because we cut them out of the investigation. He doesn't have one of your fancy phones, so the only way he knows what we're up to is if someone tells him or if he follows us. Maybe Jax didn't tell him."

Ronan sighed. "Good point. Does this mean you've decided he is connected to the assassination attempts?"

"I don't know what it means, but I intend to find out. As soon as this is over, we should have a sit-down with Vaughn and find out what he's been up to."

We made it out of the parking garage and back onto the highway. On the way over to the Palace Theater, I didn't spot the Suburban again, which must've meant we lost him.

We reached the theater and parked outside, but there were no signs that anything was out of the ordinary. The part-time security guards were there waiting for us and opened Ronan's door as soon as our car stopped. He scurried out of the car and toward the theater, with me at his back. We told the driver we'd find our own way home.

If Jax was going to make his move, it was now or never.

CHAPTER TWENTY-SIX

The theater was eerily empty. Roughly three thousand seats were arrayed on the steep incline, facing an empty stage. Our footsteps echoed, making it sound like there were twice as many of us as there were. All told, there were only five: me, Ronan, the two part-time security guards, and a guy who worked for the theater. I quickly dismissed him, slipping him an extra fifty to get lost for two hours. If this took longer, I'd have to part with more money, and the advance on my paycheck that Ronan had given me had run out.

Ronan went straight for the stage, violin case in hand. He knelt there and started to get set up for the concert. Everything had to look normal, as if Ronan really were performing a private concert. If Jax walked through the door and Ronan wasn't playing for an imaginary audience, he'd know something was off and turn right around.

I took the part-timers backstage and rolled out a map of the building. We divided it into three parts, each of us responsible for a different section. Armed with walkie-talkies and a small arsenal of handguns, as well as body armor, we set out to do our initial sweep of the theater. I took the upper sections and walked each row, checking behind every seat. I was looking for more than Jax. There might be signs that he had been there, setting up before we arrived. I was also checking for other potential security breaches and familiarizing myself with the space. It was standard procedure, or at least, that's what I told myself.

As I walked through my section below, Ronan did a check of the sound system. One of the microphones squealed, but he got it adjusted without too much trouble. The theater guy had gone into the control room and turned on a spotlight before he left, providing him with plenty of light.

I thought the violin he brought was the one I had seen him playing at his house, but that was wrong. This one looked thinner, and almost as if it were made of plastic rather than wood. Maybe it was. A long cord ran from the wider end of the violin to a piece of equipment behind him. Ronan positioned the violin against his chin and drew the bow across the strings. The sound he produced wasn't like any violin I'd never heard before. It sounded much closer to an electric guitar, but not quite. He grinned up at me, winked, and began to play.

It took me a bar or two to recognize the opening riff of AC/DC's *Thunderstruck*, and I had to admit it was actually pretty good. *Show-off.* I rolled my eyes and went back to work.

After a few rows, I found myself thinking he might be able to carry a crowd if he had the backing of a few other instruments. He was no Lindsey Stirling, but he clearly enjoyed what he was doing, and he was good at it.

I paused to clap when the song ended, and he took a bow.

"Anything?" Ronan called.

I shook my head. "Keep playing. You picked an easy AC/DC song. Now impress me."

He positioned the violin and adjusted a few settings while I finished my sweep. Next thing I knew, he'd launched into playing the first verse of *Californication*. It didn't have the energetic beat of the last number, but I had to admit that song was hard to play wrong. As he fell into the notes of the chorus, I stopped in my tracks. Was he... glowing? No, it had to be the light.

Something moved above me. I thought at first it was one of the other two security guards, but they were in other sections of the seating area, and the movement I'd seen was in the control room. I pulled my gun and crept up to investigate. The control room door creaked slightly as I pushed it open and I winced, thinking I'd lost my element of surprise. Maybe Ronan's playing had covered it. It was all for nothing, though, since the control room was empty.

A shadow shifted in one of the private booths, and I spotted him. "I've got eyes on our target. Continue as normal."

"Do you need backup?" David asked.

"Negative. Stay where you are, in case he jumps down. Let me know if he moves. He's in one of the private booths, high and stage-right."

"Copy that. I'll keep an eye on him."

I slid out of the control room and rushed out of the

main seating area as quickly as I could to head for the stairs that would take me to the balcony. Taking them two at a time, I crept up with my gun pointed at the floor.

Jax stood with his back to me, peering through the scope of a rifle. He had a perfect shot. Why hadn't he taken it yet? Maybe he thought he'd let Ronan finish his song. Or maybe he'd been waiting for me. I held my breath and closed on him, slowly raising my gun until it was even with the base of his skull. When I was close enough that he couldn't possibly dodge the bullet, vampire or not, I said, "Take your finger off the trigger, Jax."

"Or what?" His voice came out raspy. "You'll shoot me in the back? Come on, Callie. Where's your honor?"

"Then turn around so I can shoot you in the face."

Jax's finger relaxed on the trigger. He lifted his hands in surrender and slowly turned to face me. "Well? You going to shoot your old pal or what?"

I shifted my grip on the gun, my mouth suddenly dry, pulse racing in my ears. "Not if you don't make me."

Jax and I stared each other down, waiting for the other to make a move. Ronan's playing drifted up from the stage. Could he see us having our standoff, or was he so lost in the music, he had no idea what was going on around him?

"It doesn't have to be like this," I said. "You can still walk away." *Please, Jax. Don't make me shoot you.*

"Only you would think that's still an option." His hand moved so fast I didn't get the chance to react until his palm was already against my wrist, pushing the gun aside.

I pulled the trigger, but the shot went wide. The boom of gunfire shook the theater like thunder, and Ronan finally stopped playing.

Jax lunged forward. I thought he was going to go for my throat, but instead, he hit me with a headbutt that left my vision blurry. Pain exploded inside my skull. I stumbled back a step, my limbs suddenly unresponsive.

He spun and ran for the balcony. With one hand, he gripped the railing and vaulted over it to land in one of the aisles below.

I shook away the pain and ignored the copper taste of blood in my mouth to run to the banister and lean over. He might've been able to survive that fall, but if I jumped after him, I'd break both my legs.

Jax stood and drew a handgun from where he must've hidden it in his pant leg, pointing it at Ronan. The part-timers were fumbling to get their guns up and respond. Jax was going to shoot Ronan, and there wasn't a damn thing I could do about it.

"Jax, stop!" I screamed, but it was no use.

The thunder of gunfire growled through the theater as Jax pulled the trigger.

Time slowed. I knew I had to do something, but I was trapped in the balcony. By the time I made it down-stairs, it would be too late to help Ronan. I had one chance, and it was a hell of a long shot, considering my powers had been elusive at best. What choice did I have, though?

I reached for the icy magic that had let me freeze the vampire in the parking lot. It hadn't answered my call when I'd tried to summon it before, but this time I felt it lurking just beneath the surface. I coaxed it out in a blast of wintery cold and thrust it into the bullet's path, squeezing my eyes tightly closed.

The air crackled and popped with power. Ronan let out a shout.

I opened my eyes.

The floor around Jax was covered with crystallized chunks of ice at least a foot high. His feet were encased in more ice that stretched as far as his knees. His outstretched hand was also frozen in a block of ice, rendering the gun useless. Frost trailed out from that, coating the seats of a whole section. Chunks of ice filled the air, forming a line in front of Jax that thinned out the farther away from him it moved. Encased in a small frozen bubble at the end of the line, just inches from Ronan, was the bullet Jax had fired.

There was no time for me to admire what I'd done. I pushed away from the rail and sped down from the balcony. Jax would be trying to pull himself free, and he was strong. If he got loose before Ronan got to safety...

"Get Ronan out of the building!" I shouted into the walkie talkie as I ran, but I must've bumped the frequency because the only answer I got back was static. With a curse, I threw the walkie talkie down and sped around the corner to burst through the theater doors.

Jax had pulled his hand free of the ice and was working on his legs. My two part-timers had closed on Jax. He had one of them by the throat, and the other was cradling a hand that seemed like it was attached wrong. Jax must've broken his wrist when he came too close.

"Get out of here!" I shouted, and the guard with the broken wrist retreated.

The vampire threw the other guard, and his unconscious body flopped over several rows of seats before it came to a stop, rolling into an aisle. I pointed my gun at

Jax, but he tore himself from the ice just as I pulled the trigger. The block of ice exploded when my bullet hit it.

Jax bounded up the aisle toward Ronan in a straight line. I had a clear shot, but that meant shooting him in the back. Did I really want to shoot a friend in the back? *He's not your friend*, I reminded myself. *The Jax you knew was gone. You left him in Iraq. If you don't shoot right now, Ronan is a dead man.*

I held a picture of Jax in my mind. In it, he was smiling while telling a joke. He wore fatigues, his helmet, and carried the standard-issue rifle. He looked happy. That was the Jax I knew. That had to be the Jax that I remembered.

I held my gun steady, pulled the trigger, and closed my eyes.

The shot echoed through the theater, followed by silence. I cracked open an eye to find Jax face-down in the aisle, a stone's throw from being able to jump on-stage and get to Ronan. If I'd held out for a moment longer, he would have.

I lowered my gun and ran to Jax's side, dropping to my knees to check on him. With a grunt, I turned him over on his back.

Jax's hands shot up and wrapped around my neck, squeezing off my air. I stared into his bloodshot eyes. They held no hint of recognition, no sign of humanity. It was as if Jax's very soul was gone, replaced by this monster of violence and hunger.

I clobbered his arm, trying to free myself. When that didn't work, I resorted to striking his elbow. Darkness closed in at the edge of my vision.

"Callie!" Ronan shouted.

A second later, his violin smashed into Jax's head, and the instrument broke in two. The pressure around my throat released and Jax sprang up and spun on Ronan, hissing like a feral cat. Ronan dropped his bow and backed away, eyes wide with terror.

Jax stalked after him, relishing his fear. "I was only going to kill you because they told me to. Now, I'm going to do it for fun."

I need to stake him like I did the vampire at Kloud9, but with what? I searched the ground. This was a theater. There weren't going to be sharpened sticks of wood lying around. My eyes fell on the violin bow Ronan had dropped. I ran for it, grabbed it, and raised it to drive it through Jax.

He turned around at the last second and grabbed the bow in his fist. "When are you going to learn you can't sneak up on me, girl?"

"Don't call me 'girl!'" I twisted the bow and the wood snapped, leaving a jagged tip that I plunged into Jax's chest.

His eyes went wide, his body rigid.

I leaned forward, putting all my weight behind the makeshift stake, pushing it slowly into Jax's chest.

He staggered back a step and looked down at the violin bow sticking out of him, then wrapped his hands around it as if to pull it out but stopped. The look he gave me, it wasn't anger. All the rage and hate had drained from his face. The vampire beast was gone, and I got one last glimpse of the man Jax had been before he whispered, "Thank you," and fell to the floor.

CHAPTER TWENTY-SEVEN

The police came because someone had reported gunshots in the area. By the time they arrived, however, Jax's body had turned to ash. All that remained of him was a pair of bent dog tags that I scooped up and pocketed before anyone could see.

I was left to make up a story, explaining how my gun had gone off during a routine training exercise. The cops were understandably irritated over being called for nothing, but it was better than trying to explain what had really happened.

As the police were wrapping things up and getting ready to leave, Vaughn and his entourage arrived. Apparently, he'd found out where they were from the police and come to assure Ronan that none of this would fall back on him.

"If there's any official paperwork, my office will make sure it disappears," Vaughn said, walking alongside Ronan.

Ronan paused in the aisle to pick up the pieces of his broken electric violin. "I'm sure you will because if any of this lands on me or my court, I'm going to make your involvement public."

Vaughn raised an eyebrow. "My involvement?"

"Are you going to stand there and tell me you had no idea who Jax was or what he was up to?" Ronan straightened up and gave Vaughn a doubtful glare. "Our two peoples almost went to war over this, a situation you claimed to be investigating. Either you're very bad at your job, Vaughn, or you didn't want to find out who was behind the attempts on my life."

The vampire folded his hands behind his back. "I made every reasonable attempt to assist in this situation. You and Miss Hart pushed me out of the investigation at a crucial stage. Had you involved me more, I might have been able to deduce his involvement. I publicly disavow any knowledge whatsoever of Jax's actions and his existence. There are many vampires in the world, Ronan, and I simply cannot keep track of them all. That does not make me bad at my job. It makes you and Miss Hart bad at communication and teamwork."

"I think we make a pretty good team," Ronan said, raising his hand for a high five.

I slapped his palm. "Hell yeah, we do. And you owe me another steak dinner."

"Another?" he asked, turning to me with a frown. "I played what you asked."

"I must've missed your Metallica number, then."

"Damn," Ronan muttered. "I knew I forgot one. I can play it for you later."

I picked up what was left of the broken bow and gestured at his shattered violin. "Unless you've got another of those stowed away, I think it's going to be a while. I like my steaks medium-rare."

Vaughn raised his chin. "In any case, I suspect that, having captured and dealt with the assailant, you will be telling the winter queen I had nothing to do with it. Unless, of course, you have irrefutable evidence to the contrary?"

Ronan and I exchanged glances. "I know you're behind this," I said. "Someone had to be funding Jax. He didn't have the cash to buy the guns and equipment I saw him with. He certainly didn't have the resources to travel to New York. The way he was talking, someone hired him to do this, and the only one who stood to gain anything from starting a war with the fae was you."

"Can you prove your outrageous accusation, Miss Hart?"

"No," I admitted. "And it's a good thing I can't because if I could, Mab would crush you like the cockroach you are."

"Bold words for an unaligned fae." Vaughn smiled and stepped back. "Now, if you'll excuse me, I have actual work to do."

He turned his back on us and walked away.

"He's going to be trouble in the future," I told Ronan.

"I certainly don't think that's the last time our paths will cross."

Ronan was right. We might have stopped Vaughn from starting a war this time, but I couldn't be there every time he tried to stir up trouble. That was the problem with people who wanted war; eventually, they got their way.

My watch beeped, reminding me another hour had passed. We were inching toward the deadline Mab had given us. "Ronan, we still need to get back to Mab."

"Say no more." He tossed the broken violin into the trash can in the corner. "I'm ready to go."

On the drive across town, I considered everything that'd happened. I'd taken this job to make a difference, and in the hope that I would get answers about what I'd seen in Iraq. I'd gotten more than I'd bargained for. Not only had I found out that vampires were real—and deadly —but that I was half-fae. There was a whole new world for me to learn about—new people, new places, new rules.

Eventually, I'd have to choose a side. So far, I'd only met Mab and Ronan, both of whom were part of the winter court. There was a summer court too, but I didn't know anything about it. I reminded myself that I had to find out and soon since they too had a motive to stir up trouble. Ronan had said most fae stayed in whatever court they were born into, but I'd been born outside the court structure.

My mother must've been part of one of the courts. Or my father, I supposed. I didn't have any records for either of them. After spending my life bouncing around the foster system, I didn't even know their names, let alone anything about them. *I guess I'm going to have to go dig through old records.* To get my mother's name, I'd need my original birth certificate. That was easy enough, but that paper wouldn't tell me if she was fae.

I turned to Ronan. "Ronan, you said you knew I was part-fae as soon as you met me."

"Almost as soon as I met you," he corrected. "We weren't formally introduced until after I figured it out, though."

"Whatever." I waved a hand. "Is there a way to tell which court my parents belonged to?"

I'd assumed they must've been connected to the winter court. After all, the few times I'd managed to use my magic, it had manifested as ice. It didn't seem to me that summer fae would be throwing around ice spells.

Ronan shrugged. "Not really."

"But the spell I used back at the theater created ice."

"I don't know why your magic is manifesting in that way. It could be you're only using ice magic because of your connection to me, or because that's what you expect it to look like somewhere in your subconscious. Magic is complicated in its simplicity. I'm by no means a master, but we can get you someone to help you learn. I know a very good tutor." He pretended to pick a bit of lint off his sleeve.

"Or you could teach me."

He looked up and smiled. "Maybe, but then you'd only learn what I know. If you want to know if you're capable of more, we'll have to get you a proper teacher. That's something I can arrange, although you can't tell my mother. She won't like it."

Good, I thought. *All the more reason to do it.*

We didn't bother to go inside. Ronan could've made the portal anywhere, but he said it was easier to do it in the woods since the portal would be more stable there. It was dark out when we hiked back behind the house, but Ronan retrieved a flashlight from the glove box, and I almost always had one with me. A flashlight was never not useful.

"What if she doesn't believe me?" I asked as we trudged back through the woods.

"You'll have to make her believe you, Callie."

"Even if I don't think it's true?"

Ronan stopped. We'd reached the small clearing, but he hadn't stopped so he could open the portal. He turned to me and took my hands, meeting my eyes. I felt my heart jump into my throat.

"My mother will go to war if she suspects the vampires were supporting Jax. A lot of people will die if we go to war, Callie."

You have the power to stop that from happening. He didn't say it, but it was implied. Preventing war meant lying, at least by omission. I'd have to leave out everything I knew about Vaughn's involvement, which would leave him free to keep pushing toward war if he wanted. Ronan was right. I'd have to make her believe me. And I still hadn't asked Ronan about the summer court.

Ronan turned back to the clearing and brought out the ring he'd used to open the portal before. He slid it on, swept his hand through the air, and the shining portal appeared. When he held out his hand, I put my palm in his, and we walked through the portal together.

CHAPTER TWENTY-EIGHT

The winter knight was waiting for us as we came through the portal. Instead of transporting us into the old section of the palace as he had the first time, Ronan had dropped in right outside the throne room. Although I couldn't see the knight's facial features behind whatever mask he was wearing, I couldn't help but feel like he was glowering at us as we tumbled through. The heavy doors creaked as he pushed them open, holding them for us to walk through. One hand rested on the hilt of his sword, the threat clear.

If Mab's throne room had been cold before, it was freezing now. I hugged myself and clenched my teeth tightly to keep them from chattering. Ronan walked beside me, completely unbothered by the cold. *I have to check out the summer court anyway*, I thought. *I hope it's warmer there.*

Mab sat on her throne, a cobalt dress draping from her shoulders, sparkling in the light like sapphires. A wreath rested on her head in place of a crown, although gold thread had been twined through it. Little red balls dotted the wreath like holly berries. She would have looked festive if not for the disapproving glare she was giving us.

"I see you have returned, my son. I hope you have brought good news." Mab folded her hands in her lap.

"We have," Ronan confirmed, stepping up to the throne. He dropped to one knee. Not knowing what else to do, I mimicked his motions. "The assassin has been dealt with. The threat to my life is no more, thanks to Callie." He gestured to me.

Mab lifted her perfectly sculpted eyebrows and turned her attention to me. "And did you find the assassin was acting on his own?"

I took a deep breath. *Here goes nothing.* "There was no direct evidence linking Jax to the vampire aristocracy. While Jax was a vampire, I found nothing on his person to indicate he was working with anyone else."

That was true. The best lies always had a seed of truth. While I suspected Jax had been working with Vaughn and Meyer Securities, I didn't have proof. No matter how hard I searched his body, I would not have found any proof. That was partly due to him turning to dust shortly after I staked him, but I decided to leave that part out.

We waited for Mab to say something, but she remained quiet for a long time. Maybe she was waiting for us to continue, but I didn't have anything else to say. The result was an extended, awkward silence that seemed to bounce off the walls.

"Well?" Mab snapped after a few moments. "Do you have proof of your claim, or am I to take you at your word?"

I looked at Ronan, who nodded. "May I approach the throne?"

Mab sat up straighter, and the winter knight took a step closer. "You may," said the queen.

I rose and took my phone from my pocket. There was no service in the winter palace since we weren't on Earth anymore. However, I didn't need service to access the camera's gallery. I climbed onto the dais with Mab and brought up the photos I'd taken of the pile of ash that was Jax. "This is all that's left of him. I questioned him as best I could, and his testimony didn't indicate higher involvement."

Mab yanked the phone from my hands and leaned forward, scrolling through the series of photos I'd taken. I don't know why she felt the need to look at all of them. Most of them were just blurrier versions of the first one, yet she hovered on each one, scrutinizing every pixel. "What about you?" she asked. "Do you believe he was working alone or that he had the support of the vampire aristocracy?"

"What I believe isn't important, is it? You need evidence to go to war."

Mab's bitter laughter bounced off the throne room walls. "Girl, I could go to war because I felt like it." She handed my phone back to me. "Fortunately for you, I find it to be a huge inconvenience. Going to war means sitting on a war council, meeting with generals, and coordinating battle plans, none of which I wish to do. However, Ronan has asked me to trust your judgment. If I am placing my faith in you, then your opinion holds weight."

"I believe this attack was an isolated event. The

vampires do not want war any more than you do." It was another near-lie. Since there were probably some vampires who didn't want war, I could choose to believe they were in the majority and that Vaughn represented a minority. I just had to hope the queen bought it.

Mab snorted, satisfied. "Good. Then we can put this whole matter to bed, and everything can get back to normal."

I bowed and retreated down the stairs.

"Of course," Mab said as soon as my foot touched the bottom stair, "there's still the matter of your choosing a court. The law says you must state your allegiance by your twenty-eighth birthday, and according to my records, you have already celebrated your twenty-eighth birthday, Ms. Hart. However, I must acknowledge your case is unusual. You've only just now discovered your heritage, and must be allowed time to consider your options." Her fingers curled, clawing into the armrest of her throne as she spoke. "I will give you thirty days, Callie Hart. At the end of your thirty days, you will return here and announce your decision."

"Even if I decide to join the summer court?" I shouldn't have pushed her, but I needed to know for sure that I would be walking into a trap.

The armrests creaked under the weight of Mab's fists. "You will be granted safe passage upon your return. Consider it payment for what you've done for my son. You two are dismissed." She waved her hand and looked away.

Ronan and I turned to make our exit. The winter knight, however, stepped into our way. Ronan narrowed his eyes at the knight. "Step aside, Sir Knight. We have been granted permission to leave. I have no quarrel with you."

The knight stood there, an immovable force as emotive as a slab of granite. Ronan and the knight stared each other down for a long moment before the knight finally stepped aside and allowed us to pass.

"What was that about?" I asked Ronan when we reached the hallway.

"The winter knight and I have history. It is nothing you need to worry about. He's not a security threat to me."

I hope not, I thought as Ronan opened the portal to take us back. The last person I'd ever want to fight was that creepy knight.

I waited in Ronan's living room while he filled out my first paycheck. In the future, we'd set everything up for direct deposit, but for now, I'd be thankful for whatever I could get. All I wanted to do was go back to the loft, order a pizza, and pass out for three days straight. Ronan had only given me tomorrow off, though, so I'd have to pull myself together to be back at work the next day. Maybe I wouldn't have to fend off any more vampire assassins for a while. A girl could hope.

Sam was sprawled on the sofa behind me, snoring with their mouth open. Guess they were worn out too. It'd been a long night for all of us.

I glanced out the window and sighed. We'd lost most of the evening to the police investigation and our trip into the fae realm. It was edging toward midnight now. The silver lining of being out so late was that traffic wouldn't be bad. If I'd learned anything from the last few days, it was to focus on the positives. That and we should upgrade our security, and probably change our locks.

Ronan held the check out to me. "I'll get everything set up, so this process is automatic next time."

"I appreciate it." My fingers closed around the check and pulled, but Ronan didn't let go. Our eyes met.

"She tried to compel you to tell the truth, you know."

"Who did? Mab?"

Ronan nodded and finally let go of the check, his forehead creased with worry. "You just shrugged it off as if you didn't even notice. I've never seen someone dance around her questioning like that. She's probably beside herself right now, trying to figure out who you are."

"Maybe I'd better get on that before she does." I folded the check in half and tucked it into my pocket. "But first, I need food and sleep. No offense, Ronan, but you're going to have to get through the night without me protecting your ass."

"You're always welcome to stay. There's more than enough room."

I raised my eyebrows.

"I meant in the guest room, Callie, but if you want to go check under my bed for monsters, I wouldn't say no."

I rolled my eyes and kicked Sam's ankle.

Sam sat up, choking on a snore, and shouted, "Van Gogh! Rembrandt! Monet! Oh, it's you."

"Come on, Sam. Get up. We're going home."

Ronan held the door for us, leaning on it. He stopped me just before I stepped out. "Are you going to be okay,

Callie? What you did for me tonight? I know it wasn't easy."

I considered that for a moment before nodding. "Yeah, I'm good."

He nodded. "So, about that steak dinner. I know you're probably sick of my face right now, but I thought since tomorrow is your night off, we could actually enjoy it."

I laughed and shook my head. "I'll take a rain check on that. No offense, but I think I need a full day off."

Ronan seemed disappointed but nodded. "Rain check it is."

Sam yawned all the way home but refused to fall back asleep. It was just as well. Our loft was only about twenty minutes away, and we were making good time. "So, what do you want to do for food?" they said while yawning. "We could hit a drive-thru or order something in, or even brave one of the stores if you're feeling up to it."

"It's your night to cook," I reminded them.

"Damn." Sam dropped their arms into their lap. "Order in it is, then."

We arrived back at the loft just before midnight. There was a pizza place nearby that delivered until two. Sometimes, living in a college town was not so bad. While Sam dragged themselves to the bathroom to splash water on their face, I went to charge my phone so I could call the pizza place, pausing when I glanced at the door. Someone had slid an envelope underneath it. I must've missed it when I came in.

"Sam, did you forget to pay your part of the rent again?" I called as I went to fetch it.

"No, why?"

I picked up the envelope. There weren't any stamps on it, and the only writing on the outside was my name in curling letters. Something about the envelope gave me an awful feeling in the pit of my stomach. I locked the door and put my back to it before I opened it.

Inside, I found a letter scrawled in the same handwriting from the envelope.

Dear Miss Hart,

You impress me. It is rare indeed to find someone with your skills, and rarer still for that person to be aware of the supernatural world and their place in it. I am sure that Ronan McCalister has offered you an impressive salary with generous benefits. Meyer Securities is prepared to double whatever he's offering and provide you with a generous travel stipend, as well as a larger staff.

I didn't bother to read farther. I didn't need to. The rest of the letter was probably more corporate bullshit. If Vaughn thought he could buy me, he hadn't learned anything from our encounter. I crumpled the letter and tossed it in the garbage bin along with the envelope, hoping that was the last I'd hear from Vaughn Meyer.

"What was that?"

I turned and found Sam behind me. They had thrown on a fresh shirt and run a brush through their hair.

"Nothing," I replied, closing the cabinet. "What do you want on your pizza? Same as usual?"

Sam snorted and dug out their phone. "Forget that. I'm ordering. Last time I let you put in the pizza order, they left the sauce off."

"I told them to, Sam. I don't like tomato sauce."

"It's not pizza without tomato sauce," Sam grumbled and dialed the pizza place.

For once, I let them win the argument. I had a more important task on my mind.

While Sam put in the pizza order, I retreated to my bedroom, where I retrieved a small box from under my bed. In it, I'd stored the few mementos I had from my time in the service, including photos, a worn paperback that'd belonged to one of our squadmates, a watch, and a few other knick-knacks. I moved everything aside and gently placed Jax's dog tags next to a photo of our unit. In it, everyone was smiling into the sun, but Jax had the biggest smile of all. That was how I'd choose to remember him.

"Hey, Callie, they're out of pepperoni," said Sam, leaning on the doorframe. "You still want that pizza?"

"You know what? Why don't we go out tonight?" I put the lid on the box and slid it back under the bed for safe-keeping.

If you enjoyed this adventure with Callie Hart, you may also enjoy Bailey Nordin's story in the WereWitch series, also from Renée Jaggér.

If Were tradition forced you to marry at twenty-five, would you do it?

Bailey Nordin is feeling the stress of pack obligations arriving too soon in her life.

She prefers working on cars to going on a date.

A good fight is just a morning's workout, and Bailey's sarcastic wit has killed any chance of a love life.

Her future isn't looking bright.

Roland is on the run from three powerful witches who want him for...*what he can provide.*

Trying to hide from the witches, he ends up in the middle of a town so small, it's hard to find it on a map.

She's a Were, He's a wizard. He could be her ticket out of her problems—if she believed in magic.

Massive changes are coming down from the heavens, and Bailey Nordin is the Were in the middle.

Will she figure out how to break from tradition?

"It's like Romeo and Juliet... A Were and a wizard fighting kidnappers, gods, and a mysterious government agency that is trying to hide the paranormal from society.

You know what? It's actually nothing like Romeo and Juliet.

Except no one wants those two together, especially the witches."

<u>AVAILABLE ON AMAZON AND IN KINDLE UNLIMITED!</u>

NOTE FROM RENÉE

APRIL 15, 2020

You made it! Here we are again at the end of this, the first in a new series! Thank you so much for reading this far.

We are living through a momentous time for our country and our world. Momentous is usually used in the positive sense, and while things are dire indeed out there, I see amazing new practices such as widespread working from home and becoming a community again coming out of all this. Sue me, I'm an optimist.

I in no way mean to downplay the sufferings people are experiencing on a daily basis, but if the Angel of Death (or even serious illness) passes over you and yours likely living on mac and cheese and having no toilet paper (all those old phone books had to go somewhere, go find them!) are hopefully the worst you are going through. If your family has been affected, I am sincerely sorry.

What's changed for me? Almost nothing! I can still be glared at by an arrogant cat, and there is no lack of coffee in the world. Jo watches my every move and demands to go on walkies regularly. What else is there? It's easy to social-distance in the woods of Oregon, and although they don't deliver, both Starbucks and the best fish taco place have takeout, so life is good. Have to take that new red Jeep somewhere.

Seriously, authors work from home, so for many of my ilk, not much has changed.

Oh, wait, one thing has: I've begun this series! As if the WereWitch series wasn't enough, Callie and Ronan and Sam sprang into my mind one day, and now here they are! (In case you are wondering, Bailey and Roland will be back in a mega-adventure in May. If you haven't seen the Were-Witch series, check out *Bad Attitude* (WereWitch Book 1 on Amazon.com. Read it for free with Kindle Unlimited.)

Until we meet again, wash your hands, wear your mask, and don't touch your face! (Pro tip: don't attempt to eat fish tacos while wearing a mask. I can still smell the cole slaw after two washes.)

But before I go, I especially want to thank my advance reader team, especially Paul, who is both a guard and former military (Marine), and Rachel for their amazing suggestions and clarifications. They helped make this book (and every book) its best.

I hope you enjoyed Callie's and Ronan's adventure. They will be back. And if you get a moment, drop me a review, please. Those are the lifeblood of any writer. We appreciate you!

Until next time,

Renée

I COULDN'T DO THIS WITHOUT YOU!

Thanks to my early readers, you rock!

Jeff Eaton, Diane L. Smith, Dorothy Lloyd, Misty Roa, Debi Sateren, Jeff Goode, Paul Westman, Deb Mader, Jackey Hankard-Brodie, Dave Hicks, and Peter Manis

CONNECT WITH THE AUTHOR

Renée Jaggér Social

Website:
https://reneejagger.com/

Facebook Here:
https://www.facebook.com/reneejaggerauthor/

BOOKS FROM RENÉE

The WereWitch Series
Bad Attitude (Book One)
A Bit Aggressive (Book Two)
Too Much Magic (Book Three)

The Callie Hart Series
Thin Ice